Alley Rat

Colin Youngman

Copyright © 2018 Colin Youngman

All rights reserved.

Copying and reproduction, in any form, is prohibited without the express permission of the author.

ISBN: 978-1-983-336-799
ISBN-13:

DEDICATION

For Stephen, Steven and another Stephen
Mark
Anthony
&
Chris
Thanks for your interest, support and good-natured banter
(at least, I hope it's good-natured).

CONTENTS

	Acknowledgments	i
1	Monday 8th April: Day One	3
2	Day Two	8
3	Day Three	13
4	Day Four	17
5	Day Five	22
6	Day Six	26
7	Day Seven	30
8	Day Eight	35
9	Day Nine	43
10	Day Ten	49
11	Day Eleven	58
12	Day Twelve	66
13	Day Thirteen	73
14	Day Fourteen	78
15	Day Fifteen	84
16	Day Sixteen	90
17	Day Seventeen	98
18	Day Eighteen AM / PM	103
19	The Worst of Days	115
20	The End of Days	122
21	The Best of Days	130

ACKNOWLEDGMENTS

Quotes from the works of TS Eliot courtesy of Faber & Faber.

BY THE SAME AUTHOR:

DEAD Heat

TWISTS

DEAD Lines

Brittle Justice

The Refugee

A Fall Before Pride

MONDAY APRIL 8TH
DAY ONE

Months of grime flowed down the grille in a swirl of absolution. She was clean once more. Clean, save for the puncture wounds on her inner thigh.

The shower's stream remained relentless. And hot. Way too hot. The girl's naked flesh was beyond pink. Scalded red. Blistered. Yet she stayed beneath the spray.

She stayed because she had no choice. She hung from the wall, arms splayed, feet suspended inches above the tiled floor. The manacles bit her wrists like ferocious dogs.

The girl sensed a presence within the dense fug of steam, intuitive rather than visual. A figure, hunched as if dragging an item of furniture, loomed out of it. She heard something snake along the floor. Felt an object push beneath her feet. She took her weight on it. For a moment, she experienced blessed relief as her arms were relieved of their burden.

"Why?" she managed to ask, her voice hoarse through cracked and suppurated lips. She received no reply. Just the sound of heavy breathing amidst the torrent of near-boiling water.

She tried again. "Why me?" The girl found it difficult to see. Was it the swollen lids or the tears in her eyes? She couldn't be sure. "And why now, you rat?"

The girl flinched as the figure spoke for the first time. "April is the cruellest month."

A switch flicked. The convector heater beneath the girl's feet sprang to life. She saw a flash, heard a bang, and for an instant felt every nerve of her body come alive as she began her dance. Then came the smell. A burning smell. The smell of burning flesh. Her own burning flesh.

God's mercy released her.

**

Patsy MaGill isn't Irish.

He follows Celtic, loves a Guinness and prefers whiskey to whisky – but Irish, he's not.

He's never been to Belfast, only spent a single day in Dublin (watching rugby) and doesn't know the Giant's Causeway from Jolly Green Giant sweetcorn. Yet, every day at work, he's greeted in the same fashion.

"Hey, Patsy. What d'ya call an Irishman who keeps bouncing off the walls? Rick O'Shea!"

Patsy accepted the high-five offered by his colleague with bored resignation. "Good one, that, Saul. Better than Friday's," he yawned.

"Got much on today?" Saul asked as he loaded the second of two mugs with granulated coffee.

"What? Apart from the six things left on my 'to do' list from last week Don't know yet. PC's still booting up."

"Christ. The IT in this place is a bummer. Gets worse by the day." Saul flipped the tap on the communal kitchen's boiler and held a mug beneath it. "I've got a two-hour session with the Chief Exec. Suspect she's going to ask me to head-up the Peterborough plant relocation project."

"Nice one. Piss-poor pubs down there, by the way."

"Begorrah and bejabers, Patsy: beer's beer. Doesn't matter where you drink it." Saul turned his back to the swing door, put the sole of his shoe against it and pushed it open.

"Oh – and Saul," Patsy shot back, "Just remember the difference between a vulture and a CEO, won't you? A vulture has the decency to wait 'til you die before eating you."

He heard Saul laugh as the door swung shut.

Patsy admired Saul for his ambition; something which had deserted Patsy long ago. At forty-four, he had already reached his level of incompetence. He gave 100%, but not an ounce more. He worked his full day, but not a minute more. And he took home a pay packet adequate for his lifestyle, but not a penny more. He was quite happy that way.

He filled the cafetiere that would keep him stocked for little more than the first hour of his day and slowly depressed its plunger. As he did so, he caught sight of his reflection in the chrome. Realised he hadn't shaved. Again. He ran his free hand over the stubble, grateful he wasn't the one meeting with Melissa.

Rumour had it, Melissa Beacham was an efficient but ruthless cow. He'd heard that was being disrespectful to cows. And, no-one knew whether she was particularly efficient. He guessed she was but, because she surrounds herself with people who are - people like Saul – he didn't know for sure.

He sauntered back to his workstation, muttering 'good morning' to colleagues as he passed them with the insincerity of a cheesy game show host. The PC still wasn't fully loaded when he got back to his desk. A couple of post-it notes had been left on his monitor screen. He peeled them off and read them. He crumpled one up and tossed it in the wastepaper bin while affixing the other to the bottom of his to-do list. 'Make that seven,' he mumbled.

The screen finally displayed the EcoHug logo and asked for his password. He typed the ten-digit nonsense word with his non-dominant hand whilst pouring coffee with his left. He hooked a foot around the chair and wheeled it to his desk.

As always, he went straight to his e-mail inbox and waited for the folders to reveal themselves. Thirty-two new messages. Jeez. He left the office at 5.30 on Friday night and, he checked his watch, by 7.45 Monday morning there were another thirty-two e-mails. 'At least someone's got less of a life than I have,' he thought.

He scanned the left-hand sidebar. Three e-mails had red exclamation marks alongside them. He made a note of them on the foot of his to-do list. Next, he switched his gaze to the right-hand bar. Four showed red-flag alerts, meaning he'd already missed the response deadline. Patsy saw no point wasting time on these. He dragged them into an ever-growing pending folder. For pending, read forgotten. They'd never get looked at again.

Finally, he sought out those that were corporate messages, Headline Briefings and any marked 'For Info. Only.' He deleted them all without opening.

He was left with nineteen needing attention. Just about manageable. Another message winged its way to the top of the list as he watched. Twenty. He'd known worse days.

Patsy pulled out an apple from his drawer. Took a noisy bite from it. Opened his Calendar items.

"Shit."

He was late for an early morning conference call. Patsy had one every day, yet every day he forgot about it. He dialled into the conference, donned a set of headphones, and slipped into an empty meeting room to speak in privacy.

Patsy was still deep in conversation when Saul Benton stomped back to his desk. Any other day, Saul would have popped his head round the door, cup a hand to his mouth, and imitate the fire alarm just to annoy Patsy; just for the hell of it. Not today. Not after what he'd just heard from Beecham. Yep, it was Melissa earlier today, but now it was Beecham. Or worse.

He slumped into his seat, massaged his temples and punched the desk. "Bitch. Bloody horse-faced bitch." He ripped a few pages from a notepad and screwed them into a ball. Pitched it against his monitor screen. Tore out another sheet. Scrawled BITCH on it so vigorously his pen penetrated the page. He shredded the sheet into confetti.

"You'll regret this, Beecham. I'm telling you, you'll regret it."

**

Patsy sauntered back to his workstation, surprised to see Saul sitting back-to-back to him.

"You back already?"

"No, I'm still with Beecham. Yeah, I'm back. What does it look like? And you say you're not Irish. Are you sure about that?"

"Sorry, Saul. Just I wasn't expecting you two to be finished so quickly, that's all."

"Yeah, well. Life moves in different directions sometimes. She didn't want me. Can you believe it? Don't think a woman's ever said that to me before." He offered Kerri sitting opposite an exaggerated wink and received an eye-roll in return. Saul ran a hand through his sandy hair. "Never mind. Onwards and upwards." He turned his focus to his computer screen.

"So what happened," Patsy continued, lobbing the browned apple into a bin. "Was she called away to something?"

"Leave it, Patsy, ok? No, like I said, she didn't want me. I don't mean she didn't want me for a meeting; I meant she didn't want me for the project full stop. Sheesh, can you imagine that? She must be hormonal. That's the only explanation."

Kerri opened her mouth then thought better of it.

"I saw that. What were you about to say?"

Kerri kept her eyes on her screen. "Nothing."

"You were about to say 'nothing'? That's a strange thing to say: 'Nothing'. Come on. Spit it out."

"You know, Benton. You're a sexist bully sometimes."

"What do you mean?"

"All passive aggressive. Not letting things lie. Joking about periods and stuff. It's not nice, it's not right and it's certainly not funny."

"Don't tell me: you're on yours as well, right?" He guffawed, oblivious to the embarrassed silence hanging in the air.

Patsy leant back in his seat. "Ok Saul. Give it a rest, yeah?"

"Et tu, Brute? I never had you down as a feminist apologist, if there is such a thing, but ok. I'm sorry, right?"

"Don't need to apologise to me." He nodded across the desk. "Kerri might appreciate it, though."

Saul thought about it for a moment. Sighed. Ran his hand through his hair again. "Yeah. I guess you're right."

He extended an arm across the desk towards Kerri. As Kerri took his hand, he bent forward to kiss hers before working his way up her arm like Gomez Adams. Kerri couldn't help laugh. "You're incorrigible."

"Incorrigible? Wow, Patsy, you hear that? Incorrigible. They're even using long words now. And in the right context, too." He winked again. "I'm impressed." All parties laughed, tension diffused. For now.

**

Patsy MaGill liked Saul. His loud, almost boorish approach to life was a direct contrast to Patsy's own yet they hit it off, mostly.

Patsy had been the one to train Saul when he joined the company four years ago. Now, two promotions later, Saul was his senior. Not his boss, barely higher in rank, but to the company he was Patsy's superior in every way. Earmarked for great things and due another promotion, his only enemy was his own mouth.

Although Patsy had long since been left in the wake of his ambitious mentee, he still felt the need to guide his apprentice. There remained an unspoken bond between them. When Saul's dalliance with a client became public knowledge and his wife had thrown him out, Patsy was the one to pick him up. When his next girlfriend found out about his affair with an air stewardess he'd met on a business trip to Luxembourg, Patsy had taken him in. When the air stewardess got sick of him, Patsy plied him with enough drink to satisfy Dean Martin.

In return, Saul had kept Patsy's spirits up through troubles of his own. When Patsy found the growth in his abdomen and others had fussed and told him it would be benign, and everything would be ok, Saul helped because he was the exact opposite. He didn't say a word, was as irreverent as always, and carried on as if nothing had changed.

Patsy smiled at the memory, his hand reflexively resting on his stomach. Only now, with Saul finally settled with 'the one' and his own health scare behind him, had they drifted apart. Sure, they still wound each other up as jovially as ever at work, but their relationship stopped there. They were colleagues rather than partners, acquaintances more than friends.

Things were about to change again.

DAY TWO

"R_{at}."

The killer rolled the word around the tongue; mimicked the way the victim had said it. Liked the way the victim had said it. The girl had been picked up from the gutter; a homeless drug-addict no-one would miss. Rat's live in sewers and gutters so, yes, 'rat' was most appropriate.

All serial killers have a name, the killer thought, and 'The Rat' had a nice ring to it. The thought tossed around in the killer's mind like a rowing boat in the ocean. No-one refers to rats as 'he' or 'she'. As with all creatures of revulsion, they're always an 'it'. Nice. Anonymous. Androgynous.

The killer would never again consider itself male or female. From hereon, the killer was an 'it' known only as The Rat.

The Rat already knew it was special, but the name provided affirmation. All it needed now were a few more victims so everyone else knew, too. Besides, you can't be a serial killer with only one death on your hands.

The Rat recognised there was no need for fear. Select victims with diligence and your capture remained impossible. If your prey have nobody, no-one can report them missing.

The Rat sat back in the darkness of the room and contemplated the next step on the road to redemption.

**

"Top o' the mornin' to you, t'be sure t'be sure" was Patsy's kitchen greeting from Saul today.

"Hi, Saul. I take it you're feeling a tad more chipper today?"

Saul poured boiling water into his instant porridge pot. "Life's too short. Anyway, I'm sure Melissa will soon come to her senses and see the error of her ways. If not, on the bright side, it means I'll be there for Steph."

"Good man. How long now?"

Saul though for a moment as he tore off a sheet of kitchen roll and daubed at a spillage. "Three months. I think. Not really sure."

Patsy stood aside from the door to let a couple of juniors in. "You don't know when your first-born's due? Shame on you, Mr Benton."

"Oh, I know when it's due, all right. Providing it's mine. If it's someone else's, she could've done the deed anytime."

The juniors looked at each other.

"Don't worry, girls," Saul said. "It's mine all right. She wouldn't want anyone else, would she?" He grabbed his crotch and thrust his hips forward Michael Jackson-style.

Patsy grimaced. "Didn't you get into enough trouble for that sort thing of thing yesterday?"

Saul looked genuinely astonished. "Really? You call that little disagreement with Kerri trouble? You ain't seen nothing yet. Watch…" He made a fake grab towards the boobs of the taller of the two juniors, Patsy relieved to see her giggle rather than lodge a complaint.

"Ok Mr Newhouse. Time for your breakfast and leave these two girls alone."

The tall girl looked at Patsy, her brow furrowed. "I thought you just said his name was Benton, not Newhouse."

"How's your Italiano, Saul? Care to explain it to these girls?"

Saul looked at the breasts of the taller girl, Patsy not at all sure he was checking her name badge. "Well, Denise, isn't it?" The girl nodded. "Newhouse is Italian for Casanova."

"Oh," Denise said without of flicker of recognition.

"Jesus, Patsy. Let's get on with our day and leave these two to talk about One Direction or some equally vapid topic."

"Saul…"

"Ok, ok. Chill. Sorry girls. Nice to see you, Denise. And if you ever fancy a drink after w…"

Patsy dragged Saul out the door.

**

Melissa Beecham propped her elbows on her desk, hands clasped, chin resting on extended index fingers. She hadn't reckoned on Benton's reaction yesterday. She knew he'd be disappointed but didn't think he'd storm out of her office.

She needed Benton. He was sharp, alert and exuded self-confidence. All the attributes she looked for in a potential Assistant Director. She'd spotted his potential the first time they met, at a two-day conference in London which he attended in the absence of his line manager. He'd shone like a beacon amidst the flickering candles of EcoHug's staid elite.

But perhaps she'd misjudged him. An AD couldn't react the way Benton behaved yesterday. Perhaps he wasn't AD material after all.

Melissa tucked her hands behind her head. She'd possibly just saved herself from a big mistake. If Benton hadn't stomped out the room like a scolded child, if he'd listened to the reason why he hadn't been chosen for the relocation project, she'd have offered him the Assistant Directorship already. She puffed out her cheeks, at once relieved and disappointed.

Melissa opened her desk's bottom drawer. Reached for the gin. Shook her head and closed the drawer. She swivelled her chair so she looked up at the EcoHug Pharmaceuticals logo on the office wall; the head and shoulders of a green figure above a silhouette of the UK, its arms around the nation in a protective embrace.

She closed her eyes. For a moment, she wished the arms were around her before she dismissed the notion. The CEO swung her chair with a decisiveness that surprised her. "Zoe," she said into the intercom. "Find a half-hour slot in my diary for tomorrow morning. Send out a calendar invite for a meeting. In my room."

Melissa listened as Zoe raised a query. "No, don't cancel that one. Look, we can leave it a while. Find a slot when I'm free. This time next week, perhaps. Or even first thing, if possible."

Her Personal Assistant double-checked she had the details right. "Thanks, Zoe. Yes, just the two people."

Melissa switched off the intercom, fearing she'd made another wrong decision.

**

The day passed without incident. Saul behaved himself, and Patsy got through most of the items on his 'To Do' list without interruption. He checked the time on his monitor screen, frowned, checked his watch and noticed they were out of synch.

"What time do you make it, Saul?"

"5.15".

"That's what I thought. My PC says just gone 5. I'm sick of all the problems with it. Think I'll raise an incident tomorrow. I've had enough."

"Wouldn't bother with the incident report. It'll never get done. I'd go straight to Cyrus, if I were you."

"What sort of a name's that?"

"Cyrus. As in Miley. And that's rich coming from an Englishman called Patsy MaGill."

Patsy offered a wry smile. "Ok. I'll give you that one as a freebie. Cyrus, eh? The way the IT is in here at the moment, I hope he's brought his wrecking ball. So, what's the guy's background?"

"He joined about a month back. Direct entrant Head of IT."

"External candidate, eh? Wow. Must be a bit of a whiz-kid. Can't go straight to him with a tiddling little issue like this, though."

Saul swung round to face Patsy. "Why not? I have, and it wasn't a problem for him. Mind", he added. "I know how he got the job. He wouldn't dare say no to me."

"Come on, then. Spill the beans. You know you want to."

Saul tapped the side of his nose. "More than my job's worth."

"Suit yourself. I'm not giving you the pleasure of begging. Besides, if the guy sorts this mess out, he could've lay down naked in front of Ms Beecham with a rose poking out his dick for all I care."

"Ah man. Why ask if you knew all along?"

Saul ducked as Patsy's stapler headed in his direction. "Enough already," Patsy said, pulling on his jacket. "I'm out of here. Got stuff to do tonight." He shut down his PC, locked his desk drawer and was on his feet in one motion.

"Patsy?"

"Yeah?"

"Don't fancy a quick beer, do you?"

Patsy stood for a moment. It'd been a while since they'd spent time socially. "I'd like to, Saul, but like I say – I've stuff to do."

"Can't it wait?"

MaGill looked at his friend. He saw something behind his eyes, something troubled. He sat down. Pulled his seat towards Saul. "You ok, pal?"

Saul inhaled through his nose. Thought for a moment. "I'm fine. Get yourself home. See you tomorrow, yeah?"

"If you're sure."

"Yeah. Get yerself on, won't you?" he said in a risible imitation of an Irish accent. "One last thing. A word to the wise: don't go to the bookies tonight."

Patsy furrowed his brow. "Why would I?"

"Nothing important. Just I heard Murphy lost £500 at Cheltenham. And another £500 on the TV replay."

Patsy wrestled Saul in a losing battle for the stapler before waving him goodnight.

**

The drive home was a slow one. Saul dawdled through traffic, topped up the Nissan with fuel even though the gauge registered half a tank, and mooched around a Tesco store for ten minutes. He drove into the car park of The Eagle's Landing. He drummed his fingers on the steering wheel as he inspected the pub's sign; an image of the Eagle lunar module approaching the curved surface of the moon. Finally, with a sigh, he restarted the engine and drove the last three miles home.

Saul parked out of sight behind the Leylandii. He stayed there for a while before stepping from the X-Trail. He prowled back and forth like a caged lion while he pondered his next move. He knew he had no choice, really.

Steph waited inside. Steph with the swollen belly which would change his life. Forever. Caged lion, indeed.

Meanwhile, across town, a bright orange door slammed shut.

"I'm home."

DAY THREE

It hadn't slept well. A restless night filled with dreams. Pleasant dreams of the last moments of a cruciform naked woman. Adrenalin coursed through its veins at the memory of the kill.

The Rat sat up in bed. It analysed the sequence of events in the cold light of day, playing them through its mind; savouring them as if they were a delicate morsel. The girl's final words repeated themselves in its brain.

"Why now, you rat?"

It licked its lips at the memory, saliva glinting on them in the dawn light.

"April is the cruellest month," The Rat had said. It was proud of the response. Unplanned, yet instant. And so appropriate. It was pleased with itself.

Inspiration dawned. Serial killers all have a name. It had one: The Rat. But serial killers have something else. They leave a calling card.

'April is the cruellest month.'

The Rat had found its signature.

It had to kill again. And soon.

**

The elevator door slid open to reveal Patsy mid-yawn. He stepped into the darkness of the office. Blinds drawn overnight for security purposes, an eerie timbre always met the first arrival; no movement to trigger the automatic lighting.

Patsy entered the deserted, open-plan space. One hundred and twenty desks lay unoccupied in banks of six. As he strolled down the room, the strip lighting pinged one row at a time, illuminating where he'd been rather than where he headed.

He stopped dead. One desk was occupied. A figure lurked in the gloom, black T-shirt, black jeans, long hair that had once been black, too, but was now striped grey. The man had his back to him. Patsy stood in the absolute silence and observed from a distance.

The figure hunched over a desk. It worked on something one-handed while the other hand made peculiar pinching movements, thumb to index finger. Patsy realised the figure sat at his workstation.

Furtive was the best description of the man's actions. He frequently cast sideways glances from the task he was employed on, as if looking or listening.

Patsy stepped towards him. "Excuse me. What do you think you're doing? Have you permission to be in here?"

Silence.

"I said 'what are you doing'?"

Nothing but the ping of the lighting as he approached the man.

Patsy tapped him on the shoulder. The figure flinched and shrugged away from the contact but he neither spoke nor stopped his work. Patsy spun the man around in his chair. The intruder looked away, downwards then to the side.

A quick check revealed he wore no security ID. "Ok. I'm calling security."

"You'll look silly if you do." The voice was quiet, restrained. Not what Patsy expected.

"I don't think I will, somehow. I don't know how you got in here with no ID but you sure shouldn't be here."

The figure smiled. Lines etched his face. He looked towards Patsy but aimed the glance at his chest before his eyes veered away. The man still hadn't made eye contact, yet he seemed confident enough. Smug, even.

"Don't call security, Mr MaGill."

"Give me one good reason why I shouldn't." After a beat, the man's words registered. "And how the hell do you know my name?"

The elevator bell rang at the far end of the room. The sound of voices echoed in the empty space, the cheery voices of colleagues preparing to start the working day.

The man smiled again as he cast his eyes towards the floor and made the strange pecking motion with his hands. "To answer your questions in reverse order, you've got your name on your badge and, secondly, you invited me here."

Patsy's eyes narrowed in confusion.

The man laughed, more a bark than a laugh. "I'll make it easy for you, Mr MaGill. I never wear ID. I don't need to. For your information, my name's Dilley. Cyrus Dilley. I think you'll find your kit will work just fine now."

Patsy's mouth was still agape when the elevator door slid shut and Cyrus Dilley disappeared back from whence he came.

**

Saul fastened his tie with one hand and flashed his ID to Vic on the security desk with the other. He dashed towards the elevator and shouldered open the closing doors. The other occupants greeted him with a nod. "Just made it," he smiled.

He drummed his fingers against the metallic wall as the elevator stopped to let folk out at the third, fifth and sixth floor. Saul was last to alight at the ninth.

He flicked his foppish hair back as he hurried past the conference room. Patsy was in there on one of his tele-conferences. Saul backtracked a step or two. He was about to do the fire-alarm thing – better to pretend today was just another day - when he heard raised voices. Or, at least, one raised voice.

Patsy was clearly annoyed at whatever he'd heard from his client. Not like Patsy, Saul thought. He hovered outside for a moment, head tilted towards the closed door. He couldn't make out the words, just the tone. Patsy seemed to be doing most the talking, one moment calm, the next irritated and impatient. Obviously, a difficult call. Not the moment to interrupt.

Besides, Saul had enough on his mind.

**

"You ok?" Patsy checked his watch.

"Uh-huh."

"Sure?"

"Sure I'm sure. Why'd you ask?"

"Well, it's gone 11 o'clock and I haven't heard one of your tedious Irish jokes."

Saul didn't lift his head. "Didn't think you'd be in the mood after the news."

Patsy stopped what he was doing, concerned. "What news?"

"Trinity College library's burned down. Tragic, it was. Half the books weren't even coloured in."

Patsy forced a laugh, but something wasn't right. "You still cut up about that Peterborough thing?"

Saul paused, fingers poised above the keyboard. "Nah. Bigger things go on in the world than that. I never trusted the woman, anyway. Should have expected it. The woman's a woman, after all. Now, do you mind? I've got a deadline to meet."

Saul and his deadlines. "If you'd got yourself in at a reasonable hour, you'd have bought yourself more time."

Saul Benton rubbed his forehead. "I'm allowed a bad night now again, aren't I? Shut it and let me get on."

Patsy swivelled around, about to protest. Kerri raised her eyebrows over Saul's lowered head. Mouthed 'leave it'. Patsy pursed his lips and nodded.

He turned back to his e-mails and his calendar items and his folder marked 'PRIVATE' in which he typed up the notes of his latest teleconference.

DAY FOUR

Dim streetlights, little more than orange haloes floating in a sinister shroud of fog, melded into the backdrop of abandoned and boarded-up factory units to create a miasma of despair. Somewhere in the middle distance, a single bell rang out from a clock tower; the sound muffled to a dull thud by the cloying mist.

'It was a bright cold day in April and the clocks were striking thirteen.'

The Rat smiled to itself, content in the knowledge that no Big Brother watched. A detailed circuit of the disused industrial units of The Gallows estate revealed no CCTV. No surprise there. That's why they used it. No, the only one watching was The Rat.

The Rat hung back in the shadows and observed a steady stream of vehicles meander between the two largest units. None had fog lights. Many showed no lights at all. Some lingered in the alleyway, windows foggy as the night sky, but most emerged a few moments later, one additional occupant in the passenger seat. Sometimes, two.

The alley was wider than the one in which it had stumbled upon the rancid thing in the stained sleeping bag, but its inhabitants were no less odious. The Rat spat its disdain into the gutter.

Its breath came short and sharp. The time was right. It scuttled back to its vehicle and waited for a pause in the activity. It pulled to the alley's entrance, engine idling, and watched.

Spectral shadows flitted in and out of doorways. An occasional coarse shout mingled with shrieks of laughter from the vile creatures. The Rat could stand no more. It set its vehicle into first gear and crept into the alley.

Someone was about to enter their own Room 101.

The Rat didn't have long to wait. The door flung open and a thing in a short red puff-ball dress and ripped fishnets, cocooned in the stink of stale tobacco, hopped in. "£20 to £75, depending what you're after," the thing said, her voice hoarse, bored and tired. "I'm sure you know the score." The whore forced a gap-tooth smile behind over-red lipstick.

The Rat fought to repel vomit when a hand grabbed its crotch. For a moment, the whore did a double-take. "Well, whatever takes your fanc…"

The sentence lay hanging as the ether-soaked rag covered her nose and mouth.

**

"…so, that's where we stand, gentlemen. To summarise, if we don't cut our cloth accordingly, I assure you we are royally screwed."

The suits of EcoHug grimly shuffled their papers, pushed back their plush leather chairs, and stood as one. At the head of the long table, the sole female remained seated.

"Not you." Melissa Beecham pointed across the boardroom to one of her departmental heads as if firing an Apprentice. "You stay behind for a moment."

The man sat down without offering Melissa a glance. He picked a long strand of grey hair from his Deep Purple T-shirt and inspected it between pinched fingers.

Melissa smoothed down her skirt and moved to a seat closer to him. The man angled his body away from her.

"We're overdue your first one-to-one. May as well take this opportunity since the meeting finished early. You ok with that?"

Cyrus stared at the polished surface of the table and nodded assent.

"Good. Nothing formal, you understand. I know that's not your thing. Now, you've been with us, what," she made a play of looking at notes on her clipboard, "Seven weeks now. How are you settling in?"

Cyrus glanced up, then away again as their eyes met. "I'm doing ok."

She smiled a smile which never reached her wide-set eyes. "I'm pleased. You probably realise there were other, more experienced candidates with better-rounded CVs than yours, but I'm sure you know I recruited you for certain skills you bring to the table. I wonder if you're ready to utilise those skills."

"I am."

She barely heard him, so soft was his voice. Melissa Beecham's eyes drifted to his hands, the fingers opening and closing. "Excellent. Before we discuss what it is I need from you, how do you feel your Department's running?"

"It's ok."

Melissa sucked in air between her teeth. This was a difficult conversation. She tucked a strand of black hair behind her ear and stretched a hand towards him. Realised it was the wrong move and retracted it.

"We're both on the same page when it comes to why I hired you, but running a Department requires more than a brilliant technical mind."

"You said you'd make allowances."

"I am making allowances. I'm happy for you to leave the day-to-day running of the IT Department to a delegate. More than happy. You don't need involve yourself in administration, planning, strategy – any of those things. But I need to know who you've put in charge of the routine stuff."

"Lynette Szydlowski."

"Why her?"

Cyrus sneaked a peek in Melissa's direction. "She was next in line."

"Is that the only reason? We choose the most senior suitable here in EcoHug, not the most senior."

"Of course it's the only reason. Why would I select her otherwise? She's a woman. You'll tell me I'm not allowed to say that sort of thing but it's true. I wouldn't pick a woman out of choice."

Melissa relaxed. "You're free to say those things, Cyrus. To me, in private, anyway. Didn't you learn anything from your first board meeting?"

He didn't raise his head, but Melissa saw his brow furrow.

"All my immediate sub-ordinates are men. I'm as one with you on that score."

He looked up and held her gaze.

"So, onto the assignment I have for you…"

**

Kerri Duncan scuttled up the room, 'Little Miss Hug' cup in hand. "Patsy. Patsy. Wait up."

Patsy slowed his pace. The two exchanged pleasantries on their way to the office kitchen, the place where most company communications and news was exchanged. As soon as the door swung shut behind them, Kerri's demeanour changed.

"Do you know what's up with Saul?"

Patsy regarded her as he topped up his cafetiere. "Not sure I know what you mean."

"Come on. You must have noticed. He's been different, these last few weeks."

"I think 'weeks' is over-egging it a bit. He's had a couple of bad days, that's all."

Kerri bit her lip. "I know you'll want to defend him but he's..." she searched for the right word. "Changed."

Patsy barked out a laugh. "Changed? What, you mean he's a shapeshifter or something?"

She didn't smile. "No. I mean he's behaving differently. Not himself. He's always been the most politically incorrect guy in the office, but it's always been light-hearted; said in a way no-one could take offence. But just lately, it's… it's more vitriolic. Hurtful, sometimes. I'm just worried about him, that's all. You know him better than most. Haven't you noticed anything?"

The door opened. Four others entered the cramped kitchen space. Patsy and Kerri pressed the pause button on their conversation. "Go on, you play through," Patsy gestured the others towards the facilities.

The interruption gave him time to think. He recognised one of the new arrivals as the girl Saul had accosted a couple of days ago. It got him thinking. Perhaps there was something in what Kerri said.

After Denise and friends left them alone again, Patsy chose his words carefully out of loyalty to his friend. "I think he's having a bit of a bad time at home. I don't know for sure; just a couple of things he's said. He's bound to be a bit uptight, what with the baby due soon and all. I think you should cut him a bit of slack."

Kerri tilted her head. Thought for a moment. "Yeah. I guess you're right. Keep me informed, though, Patsy, will you? I like him, you know?"

"I will. Promise." He returned her smile.

Nosey cow. She was right, though. Saul wasn't himself.

**

Waves of nausea crashed her against the rocks of consciousness.

Slowly, she raised one eyelid. Stark white lighting greeted her. The woman snapped her eye shut with a groan. 'Hangover from hell,' she thought. 'What was I drinking?'

She licked her lips, mouth as dry as a dead dog's dong. She grimaced at the taste in her mouth. Not an unusual occurrence in her line of work but this taste was different; a chalky/metallic tang. The woman felt herself retch. Swallowed it down. Took in a deep breath and held it. The air felt musty.

She puffed out her cheeks. Tried opening her eyes again. This time, she succeeded. She wished she hadn't.

The room was bare; a vast open space, once-white walls now scarred with the curved lettering of lurid purple, blue and green graffiti.

"What the…"

She focused on the cracked and grimy window pane. The sun began to rise. She realised she'd been there all night. The woman did a double take – the sun wasn't rising; It had almost set.

"Jeez. How long have I been out of it?" Her speech was slurred.

She looked away from the window, noticed her nakedness for the first time. Realisation crept into her befuddled thoughts.

Her John had drugged her.

"Shit."

She slumped back, head tilted upwards. She stared into the glare of powerful lighting. After a day of absolute darkness, the woman felt she'd been subjected to pepper-spray.

The woman went to rub her eyes - and discovered she couldn't.

She was manacled to the wall.

.

DAY FIVE

"What time will you be back tonight?" The question came from Steph Benton.

"I'm not sure. I've a lot on at the moment. I want to prove to Beecham how mistaken she was. I'm looking forward to rubbing her nose in it. She'll be begging for me before long." He caught her mood and sighed. "Begging me to lead on the relocation, I mean."

Steph picked at a fingernail. "I need you here, Saul. I'm struggling, you know."

He clicked his tongue against the roof of his mouth. "You're not the first woman to have a baby, you do realise that, don't you?"

"I'm the first woman to have your baby, though. I thought you'd show more interest; some concern."

Saul inhaled through his nose. "We'll do this later, yeah? I don't have time for it right now."

Her stare could have frozen Hell. "It's always later. 'We'll talk about this later', 'we'll decide on that later'. There's so much to do, Saul. Just about the only thing we've done is settle on a name. Our little Roland will be here before you know it. This is going to change our lives – and I'm scared."

He stood, fists clenched by his side. "Don't you think I know our lives will change? Don't you think I'm frightened? I didn't want the damn thing in the first place. Still don't, if you must know. Now, I'm going to be late. I've got work to do."

The door shook in its frame as Saul Benton slammed it shut behind him. Steph brought her knees to her chin, held her bump close, and rocked back-and-forth as torment bled from her eyes.

**

Mindful of his conversation with Kerri yesterday, Patsy angled his monitor so he could see Saul's reflection behind the overlay of spreadsheets, PowerPoint presentations and databases as he worked his way through today's chores. He needn't have bothered. He could tell Saul's mood by the rat-a-tat of fingers on keyboard.

Kerri had noticed it, too. "For Heaven's sake. What's that keyboard ever done to you?"

"Not today, Kerri. Please. Not today."

"Look, we all have our problems. I've got plenty of them. But I don't bring them to work with me."

"Correction. You've only got one problem. And that's not being able to keep your mouth shut."

She stopped what she was doing. "Right. I've had enough of this. You and me – into the conference room. Now!"

Saul gave a sarcastic laugh. "Ooh hark at her. Are you offering me outside for a fight? Patsy, you'd better hold my jacket."

"Not a chance. I'm coming too."

"Hey, I'm outnumbered here. But not outranked. Just remember who you're talking to, the pair of you."

They marched down the office, Kerri leading the way, a silence over them like mourners at a funeral. Kerri started before the door closed on them.

"I've had it, Saul. Up to here." She held a hand an inch above her head. "I want to know either what I've done, or what the hell is up with you." She leant towards him, face flushed. "And no shitting me."

"I like it when you talk dirty."

"Saul," Patsy's turn, arm resting on his friend's arm, "Cut the crap, just for once, yeah?"

Saul closed his eyes. Tried to compose himself. "Ok. I'm sorry. There's things going on you don't know about. Stuff at home. Me and Steph. The baby. And when the Beecham woman put her oar in, well – that just about topped it off. And then there's you." He stubbed a finger at Kerri.

"Right. What have I done? Come on, I want to know."

"As if you didn't know already."

"Know what? For God's sake, what?"

"You told her."

Kerri shook her head. "Told who what? You're not making any sense."

"Beecham. You told her not to offer me the Peterborough post."

Patsy watched the exchange as if it were a tennis match, head following the rally of conversation. He tried to adopt the neutral position of an umpire. "Tell us why you think Kerri would do that."

"You mean you don't know? Isn't it obvious? She wants the job herself. 'Little Miss Hug' here, always so nicey-nicey. Trying to suck up to folk. To get her tiny little self noticed because, like most the women round here, they've got a bee in their bonnet because Beecham never appoints them to any position of merit. And can you blame her? Devious things, they are." Spittle flumed from his mouth as he spoke. "All of them. Not to be trusted. But I tell you what, you can have the goddamn project. And you know why? Because you'll fall flat on your perfumed arse. You're not up to it. None of you are."

Saul ripped off his ID and stormed out. Patsy let out a low whistle. "Glad I asked," he muttered. "You ok?"

Kerri nodded but kept her head down to hide the tears in her eyes.

"For what it's worth," Patsy added, "He's definitely not himself."

**

She'd been clamped to the wall for so long she'd lost all feeling in her hands and wrists. She was cold. Cold and hungry. And she craved a cigarette.

It was far from the first time a client had tied her up. In fact, she'd long since realised it was a common male fantasy but not one shared with most wives. That's why they came to her, and a nice little earner it had been over the years. But she'd never been drugged. Or left hanging.

The woman shivered. Not with the cold this time, but at the memory of something she'd been told. By a fellow-whore with wide-set eyes and a long face. Something about being tied up and left in a room for days, only for her client to return with three business partners happy to take the freebie he offered. She brought her knees up to cover her nakedness.

A key turned in the lock and she heard the grind of a heavy bolt draw through a latch.

**

Melissa Beecham held the future in her hands. She took a slug of gin straight from the bottle and paused to take in the enormity of the task. Everything depended on her next move. The prospect both thrilled and daunted her.

Beecham stepped along the deserted corridor and boarded the elevator. Muzak seeped into her subconscious like the words of a Svengali. When the doors opened, she slipped off her heels and made her way towards a closed door.

The room she entered was dark. There was only one occupant; an occupant wondering what was to come next.

* *

With wide eyes, the whore squinted into the darkness. She knew there was a presence but it either remained still or moved silently.

"I know you're there. Listen, I know you must have had me at least once already," she said. "I don't mind if you take me again. On the house, like. But, please, do it now then let me go. Please. It's Friday night. I've money to earn." She tried to sound casual, and hoped it came out with more confidence than she felt.

The only noise came from the echo of her own voice in the concrete chamber. "Do you hear me?"

A familiar smell of sweet alcohol reached her nostrils. She groaned. "Not again."

A hand clamped the rag over her face and she drifted into oblivion.

DAY SIX

Steph stood at the sink, dishcloth in hand, staring out over the freshly cut lawn and daffodils which peeped from their beds like newly-hatched chicks from eggs. She felt Saul's arms wrap around her midriff. Steph tried not to tense, but she lost the battle. Her back straightened, her chin rose, and the slightest of shudders ran up her spine.

"Penny for them," Saul asked.

"Not sure a penny will cover it."

He hugged her a little tighter. Nuzzled her neck. Tried to breathe in her scent but only caught the apple aroma of dishwasher liquid. "Not wearing any perfume today?"

"It's Saturday morning. I'm doing housework. And no-one cares if I do or don't." Steph flung the cloth into the basin, bubbled water splashing onto the floor. "Can I get on?"

Saul released her. "Can we talk? Please? I've got some apologising to do. To lots of people. But especially to you."

"Saul, I can't take much more of this. My hormones are all over the place. I'm tired. I ache all the time. And you never notice." She saw he couldn't meet her eyes. "What's worse, you can't wait to get to the other end of the country."

"It's not you I'm running away from. It's…" he thought for a moment, "It's other things. Besides, it's my career. It's what pays for all of this." He signalled to the lavishly-equipped kitchen. "I'm thinking of you and Roland. What's best for you, how I ensure the best future for our son."

Steph took his chin in her hands. Tilted his head up. Forced him to look into her eyes. "Listen. I need you. Your son needs you. Here, with us. As a family. All 'this', as you call it, 'this' doesn't matter. We matter. The three of us."

Saul pulled away from her. Perched himself on a stool by the breakfast bar. He rubbed his forehead until it reddened. "Steph. I'm sorry. I've said some dreadful things. I even said I didn't want my own son. Of course, I want him. And I want you. But I can't clear my head, and I need to. Can you forgive me?"

If Saul thought his wife would soften her stance, he was mistaken. "I don't know. Prove it. Prove you want us. Forget all the other stuff."

"I will, I promise I'll prove it."

He wished he could remember the 'other stuff', let alone forget it.

**

Patsy sat alone in the bar and watched the clouds in his Guinness swirl like a cosmic storm.

The lunchtime kick-off played in the background, and a barmaid busied herself clearing plates from nearby tables. Patsy didn't quite catch something she said but he didn't ask her to repeat it. Why would he be interested in anything a barmaid had to say?

He continued to watch his pint, afraid to drink from it in case it interrupted the magical images forming in the darkness of the stout.

A chair screeched. Another voice spoke. "You work on the same floor as Benton, don't you?"

"Yep." Patsy said, his gaze never leaving the glass.

"Know him well? Outside of work, like."

Slowly, Patsy raised his eyes. Bald head, glasses, mid-fiftyish. He recognised him as a guy who worked security at EcoHug. "I used to, one time. Don't see much of him outside of work these days."

"Do you have a contact number for him?"

"Might do. Why?"

"Well, if you have, let him know to see Vic on Monday. I've got his ID pass. He won't get in without it."

Patsy remembered Saul tearing it off during Friday's argument. "Ok, but I think he'll know the procedure well enough." His attention drifted to the TV momentarily when a group of lads 'oohed' at the screen, the commentator's raised voice indicating Newcastle had taken a surprise lead away at Spurs. "Want a pint?" Patsy heard himself ask. He looked around. Yes, it was him who asked the question. God knows why.

The man called Vic checked his watch against the time remaining in the match. Fifteen minutes. "I'll have a quick half, ta. Haven't got long."

When Patsy returned with two half pints, he asked Vic if he drank there regularly. They exchanged humourless laughter at the realisation it sounded like a lame chat-up line. Vic explained he hadn't lived in the city long and was getting familiar with the sights and sounds.

"Not one of the more scenic parts of town, this." Patsy swigged from the pint of Guinness, then topped it up with the half. Black liquid pooled on the table where it overflowed.

"I wouldn't say that. There's some interesting architecture in the most unlikely of places." He pointed towards a cornice high up against the cracked ceiling. "Take that, you'd normally see one of those on an exterior wall. Rare to find something like that as part of interior décor."

"Thank you, Frank Lloyd-Wright."

Vic laughed; a curious falsetto at odds with his speaking voice. "Yeah, I know. Not the most interesting of subjects but I'm always fascinated by old buildings, curious side-streets, shop fronts. I'm not an expert, mind."

"You surprise me," Patsy mumbled under his breath. "Anyway," he said, changing the subject, "Shouldn't you be helping your wife in the garden or something?"

"Nah. Not married, me. The shifts I work – twelve hour days, twelve hour nights or splits of six each – isn't conducive. Besides, I never really understood women. How about you?"

Patsy regretted ever getting into this conversation. He shook his head, then checked his watch. He finished his drink in two long gulps and pretended he'd forgotten an appointment. "Excuse me, won't you? I've just remembered I need to be somewhere."

Patsy had already left by the time Vic said, "You will tell Benton, won't you?" whilst staring upwards at another obscure architectural feature.

**

Saul pressed disconnect and returned his phone to his pocket. The call had gone better than expected. He'd apologised – sort of – to Steph, and now he'd made his peace with Kerri. He wasn't sure he had anything to be contrite about but someone had to make the first move. Now, he needed to see how the land lay with Patsy.

He stepped into the fresh air, psyched himself up for his opening gambit, and speed-dialled Patsy's number. "Hi Patsy, its m…"

"…take your call right now. If you leave a message after the tone, I'll get back to you when I can."

Perhaps he was in the middle of something. Saul waited a few moments and dialled again. Same result. This time, he left a message.

"It's me, Patsy - Saul. Listen, about that drink I mentioned. I meant it. It would be good to catch up socially again. And it would be a way of apologising for last week, at work. I was a bit of a knob, wasn't I? Oh, and in case you're wondering, I've already spoken to Kerri. She was fine about it. I think. Anyway, when you get this, give me a call, yeah?" He considered closing with a joke but settled on, "See you, Patsy."

**

From the top of Mother's Mound, the grey slab of the city spread herself like a sleazy centrefold from the pages of urban decay.

Largely featureless, it could be any medium-sized city anywhere in the world. The chrome-and-glass frontage of the EcoHug administrative HQ reflected evening sunlight like a diamond in a jeweller's window. A Gothic cathedral in the foreground attracted the eye, and a ribbon of water ran along the city's eastern border. The remainder was an inner-city mass of 1960s concrete as drab as a tramp's overcoat.

Yet, The Rat liked the view. Down there lay its next victim. And the one after that, and the one after that. On the outskirts of the city, the football stadium's floodlights reminded The Rat of scrawny fingers clawing free from the surrounding mediocrity. Which reminded it. It had work to do.

The Rat hauled itself to its feet, sauntered to its car and extracted a spade from the trunk. The rest of the contents remained undisturbed.

Contents which lay like a patient etherised upon a table.

DAY SEVEN

She'd long since given up all hope. Drugged, bound, gagged, hauled naked into a car and transported to God-knows-where – she knew this couldn't end well.

She was resigned to her fate hours before she was lugged head first onto a soft surface she recognised as grass. What surprised her was the darkness. She hadn't expected it to be night-time again.

The whore braced herself. Prayed it would be quick. By the time her eyes became accustomed to the darkness, she knew it wouldn't.

She'd been dumped next to a hole. In the dim moonlight, she reckoned it to be two-and-half feet wide, eight feet long, six feet deep. She knew what it was. Her widowed father had dug plenty in his time before he'd run out on her and left her to the home.

She refused to let her killer see her fear. Wouldn't give the killer the satisfaction. So, when she felt urine soak her upper thighs, she was more disappointed than disgusted.

A shadow fell over her, depriving her of her last sight of the moon and stars. Hands grabbed her hair. Tore at the gag around her face. Her determination to remain stoic disappeared at the sight of the face grinning down at her, and the barely-human expression on it.

An involuntary scream formed in her throat. As she opened her mouth to free it, a fistful of dry dirt filled the maw. She felt herself gag. Vomit welled in her throat. It had nowhere to escape. She recognised she'd choke on her own stomach contents.

A foot rolled her over and she felt herself fall into the abyss. Parched dirt landed atop her, the sound of a shovel ladling ever more soil into her grave. The last thing she heard before her face became completely submerged was The Rat's voice.

"I will show you fear in a handful of dust."

**

Rain swept over the resting city streets, a sharp shower which came and went as quickly as a child's tears. Water pooled in omnipresent potholes.

A single car cruised the deserted Sunday-morning lanes and alleys. A traffic light changed above a faded zebra-crossing as a group of dirty-stop-out revellers meandered their way home. The driver almost tooted in disdain before realizing it would draw attention. There again, would that be a bad thing? What's the point in being a serial killer if you were so good no-one missed, found, or cared about your victims? What's the point if no-one knows you exist?

The light changed to green. Still The Rat remained motionless. An idea formed. It had a name. It had a calling card. It was time to go public.

The light changed to red. The Rat drove through it, destiny mapped.

**

"Steph said I might find you here."

Saul jumped. "Bloody hell, Patsy. I was in a world of my own there."

"So I see. I got your message. Thought I'd pay you a visit rather than call you. I've nothing better to do on a Sunday."

Saul screwed up his face. "Hmmm. Not sure that's a compliment."

Patsy laughed. "True. I meant it as one, though. Didn't quite come out right, did it?"

"Good to see you, Patsy." The wind ruffled Saul's hair. He straightened it before they exchanged handshakes. They stood on damp grass squinting into sunlight. Patsy broke the silence.

"How's things, Saul?"

Saul sighed. "I'm ok. Not 100%, if I'm honest, but ok."

"Listen, I'm in no position to lecture you on family life but don't you think you should be with Steph rather than out here? She's hurting. Frightened. Today's the first I've seen of her for over a year and she doesn't look well. She's lost her colour. Her face is pinched. Aren't you concerned?"

"She's pregnant, for God's sake, that's all. I am worried, but not about her."

"Then, what?"

Saul looked at his friend. "The thing is, Patsy, I don't know. I'm worried but I haven't a clue what about. Does that sound stupid?"

Patsy thought for a moment. "No. Not really. We all have things in our past; things that remain hidden. Things we don't even consciously hide. It's how we cope with it that matters."

Saul made a noise like a horse. "MaGill, the famous Irish philosopher, eh?"

"I'm not Irish, as well you know."

"So, I guess you'll refuse a pint of Guinness? We could always go to yours for a coff…"

"No!"

Saul held up his hands. "Whoa. Joke, my friend. I take it from that you'd prefer a pint?"

"Yeah. Sorry. It's just my house is in a bit of a state, but you got yourself a deal on the drink this time."

"Good man." Saul wrapped an arm around Patsy's shoulder and led him away, down towards the city.

Down from Mother's Mound.

**

While everyone else spent Sunday with family or friends, Melissa Beecham pored over plans and maps and strategies.

She needed a break.

She tied up her hair and padded across the deep-pile carpet of her EcoHug-sponsored apartment towards the drinks cabinet. She held a bottle of gin up to the light, shook it, and sighed at its emptiness.

Arms akimbo, she looked out the French windows, out across the canal and up to Mother's Mound.

She needed more than a break. What she needed was a drink.

**

The bar was off the beaten track, tucked down an alley between a discount supermarket and a McDonald's.

The smell of takeaways only partly hid the stink of urine in the alley, but the bar itself was decent enough. It was a drinker's bar. High ceiling, burgundy leather furniture, mahogany fittings, etched mirrors standing tall behind the optics; a man's bar.

Saul and Patsy's table was soon festooned in empty glasses and they sat in silence, small-talk spent. Inevitably, conversation returned to work.

"By the way, I bumped into one of the security guys yesterday. He's got your ID. You left it when you had your strop on Friday."

"Don't tell me – styles himself on Phil Collins but ends up looking like Danny De Vito?"

Patsy snorted at the image conjured up. "Yeah, that's him. How'd you guess?"

"Because Victor Pritchard never seems off duty, that's how. Thanks. I'll collect it from Vic the Prick when I get in tomorrow."

More silence.

"Did I tell you I met that Miley Cyrus guy, as well?"

Saul spurted beer, wiped drips from his chin. "It's Cyrus Dilley. No. What did you make of him?"

"Weird. Odd. A bit scary. And weird again."

"He's good, though."

"That's as maybe but he doesn't exactly look the part, does he? He's doesn't dress smart enough to work on the helpdesk, let alone be Head of Department."

"Beecham makes allowances."

"Allowances for what?"

Saul took a mouthful of beer, wiped away creamy froth clinging to the inside of his glass. "Ever see The Rainman?"

"Dustin Hoffman? Yeah. So what?"

"Well, that's Cyrus."

Patsy sat back in his seat. Snapped his fingers. "Of course. Makes sense now. A savant."

"Not quite. But definitely on the spectrum. More Asperger's, I think."

Patsy raised an eyebrow. "Wow. Does well to run a department. Props to him." He lifted his glass in salute and took a sip of Guinness.

"Rumour has it, he doesn't. Leaves it all to that Lynette woman. You know, the one who forgot to put enough vowels in her surname."

"Szydlowski."

"Easy for you to say.

"A woman acting as the effective head of IT? No wonder it's all gone tits up. So, what exactly does Miley do?"

Saul laughed again. "Dilley. No-one knows for sure, but I reckon it's barely legal."

"Come again?"

"Word is he's an expert hacker. Not only got into Scotland Yard's systems, he broke through the CIA firewall, too."

"You're kidding me, right? How'd you know these things?"

Saul tapped the side of his nose, a habit Patsy was beginning to find infuriating. "Never reveal your sources."

Patsy knew he'd get no further. He checked his watch. "Ok, Saul. Time you got back to that lovely wife of yours. She tells me you were late back yesterday. Better not let it happen again, for both our sakes." Saul didn't respond. "Saul?"

"What's she doing in a place like this?"

"Who?"

He pointed to the doorway. A figure stood with their back to it, looking outwards, surveying the alley.

"Melissa Beecham."

DAY EIGHT

The elevator was out of commission beyond the sixth floor. Saul Benton took the stairs the remainder of the way, three steps at a time, ID suitably collected from the oddball on security.

He arrived breathless, trying hard not to show it. Kerri Duncan was already at her desk, beavering away. She greeted him with raised eyebrows, a smile not quite rising to the surface, and continued typing.

"Are we ok?" Saul gasped.

"Uh-huh."

"Doesn't seem it."

She pressed the return key with a flourish. "No. I'm fine. I am. Just needed to get this e-mail off. I appreciated you calling yesterday. I really did." This time, her cherubic features did crease in a smile. "We'll try a bit harder from now on, should we? Both of us?"

Saul paused for a beat. Almost told her he had nothing to 'try harder' about. Instead, he nodded.

Kerri smiled. "Good. And I'm sorry if you thought I was prying. I can't help it. I'm Taurus; we're a naturally curious breed, you know."

"That tosh doesn't wash with me. I'm Cancer. Doesn't mean I've got crabs."

She wagged a finger in fake admonishment. "Now, now. Careful, Saul. So, there'll be no more sexist jokes. Promise?"

He put his hand against his heart. "I hereby swear that, from this moment forth, there shall be no more blonde jokes, no more bedroom jokes - and no more PMS jokes." Pause. "Period."

Despite her best efforts, a laugh escaped Kerri. "What are you like, Saul Benton?"

"You wouldn't have me any other way."

Beneath the façade, she thought there lay a sadness she'd not seen in him before. "Do you know, I don't think I would."

At the head of the room, Saul noticed a flustered-looking Patsy step out the stairwell and straight into the conference room.

"Those calls of his get earlier each day. Never mind, it'll give me time to Google 'crap Irish jokes.' I'm running out of them." He saw Kerri frown. "What's that look for, Duncan? I promised to quit the sexist jokes, not the Irish ones."

She took a sip from a bottle of spring water. "Fair point." She slid a sheet of paper across the desk. "Here's one I prepared earlier."

Saul scanned the page. "Kerri Duncan. Whatever would I do without you?" He blew a kiss in her direction. She pretended to catch it and brought it to her heart.

"Wa-hey. I didn't think you'd let me kiss you there."

"You're not going to change, are you?"

"Nope. Don't think I am."

She shook her head and started on another e-mail. But at least she did so with a smile on her face.

**

"What do you call an Irishman lost at sea?"

"Hmm?"

"What do you call an Irishman lost at sea?"

Patsy typed in his password. "It should get out later, though."

"What?"

"If you say so."

Saul shook his head. "I was abducted by aliens last night."

"Ok."

"They replaced my testicles with helium balloons."

"Good."

Saul banged his mug against the desk until Patsy looked up. "Ground Control to Major Patsy. I presume it was another difficult call? You're lost in another world today."

"Not really." He continued to focus on the screen as the EcoHug logo made way for Outlook.

Saul made a sibilant sound. "I get the message. Hungover. Shouldn't drink with the big boys. Ok, I'll let you get on."

"If you don't mind."

It was Saul's turn to exchange glances with Kerri. They shrugged, were about to speak, then heard Patsy groan. "Christ. That's all I need."

"What's up?" Kerri asked, taking another chug from her bottle.

"Calendar appointment popped up. Not even had a chance to load my e-mails yet. CEO wants to see me." He checked his watch. "Five minutes ago. She can wait another five. I'll get this note off first."

Saul swung around in his chair. "I wouldn't, if I were you. Especially if we've been a naughty boy. You haven't, have you?" He thought he saw Patsy colour. A trick of the light, he concluded.

"Well, we're about to find out." Patsy pinged off his note via e-mail and grabbed a clipboard, grateful he only had one flight of stairs to mount.

Patsy hoped Zoe's face would give him a clue as to how severe a rollicking he was in for but, when he entered the CEO's anti-chamber, the PA hadn't arrived for work.

He gave a tentative rap on the polished oak door and could almost hear Melissa Beecham think 'one, two, three, four; let him wait outside the door'. Right on cue, he heard her say, "Come."

Melissa was seated at her desk, head buried in paperwork. Two cups of coffee lay on a side table next to the leather sofa adjacent to her desk. "Take a seat, Mr MaGill." She gestured towards the sofa.

When she thought he'd waited long enough, she raised her head and smiled. "How old do you think I am?"

The opening gambit threw him. How the hell do you answer that one? "Mid-thirties?" Patsy erred on the side of caution.

"Close. Thirty-nine, actually. And may I ask how old you are?"

"Forty-four." He had no idea where the conversation was going.

"Exactly." Beecham's smile unnerved him. "Only five years between us. I'm CEO of the company I joined straight from University. And you – well, you're not. Why do you think that is?"

Patsy shrugged. "For starters, it's a pharmaceutical company and I don't have a degree in science."

She gave him a dismissive wave. "Irrelevant. I didn't major in science, either. I have an Arts background. Besides, we both work in the administrative headquarters. If we were in a production plant, it might be different. But you don't need a science degree to be able to work in Sales, Finance, Strategic Planning, IT or HR. No, Mr MaGill – Patsy - the difference is ambition. Ambition and drive."

Patsy stifled a yawn. His head hurt. And he could do without all this. "I was ambitious, once," he felt compelled to defend himself. "But I'm happy with what I do. Are you unhappy with my performance? Is that why you called me here?"

"Not at all. I'm here to help you regain your drive and ambition. To help you better yourself." She moved from her desk. Took up position at the opposite end of the sofa. Sipped from one of the cups. "Mm, please," she gestured to the other. "Help yourself."

"No, thank you. Anyway, what if I don't want to be bettered?"

"Nonsense." The dismissive wave again. She moved closer to Patsy. He caught a whiff of something. Alcohol, perhaps. Was she a secret drinker? His mind drifted to yesterday's encounter in The Bull. Was she checking the alley to make sure she hadn't been seen? She pressed on before he could gather his thoughts. "So, that's why I have a proposition to put to you."

"Oh-kay."

"The Peterborough project. It's yours, if you want it."

Patsy recoiled, stunned. He needed the coffee after all. He raised the cup to his lips. After blowing across the top of the mug, said, "I can't."

"You can. And you will."

A threat? He didn't know. "No, you don't understand. It's not a matter of whether I want it or not. I just…I just can't."

Beecham's face dropped for a second. "Don't tell me it's back, Patsy."

His hand shot to his abdomen. "No, no. It's clear. For now, at least."

She quickly regained composure. "In that case, I get it. It's a loyalty thing, isn't it? You and Mr Benton. Thick as thieves. You know, I respect that. I really do. That's why I prefer to work with men. But don't let that hold you back, Patsy. Just think of the opportunities, the kudos you would get. Not only that, you need a change of scenery. Fresh impetus."

"Miss Beecham. Thank you, but no. It's not possible. Not now."

The CEO stood. Walked to the window. Looked out over the city, to the canal running along its periphery. The sunlight sprinkled silver glitter along its length. Just when Patsy thought she'd forgotten he was there, she spoke. "Come on. It's a lovely day. Let's get some fresh air."

**

Kerri Duncan looked up from her PC and realised she was alone. Patsy was still with Beecham, and Saul must have been called into a meeting. She forwarded an e-mail to Cyrus Dilley containing details of the department's IT performance, only to find his 'Out of Office' message wing its way into her in-box.

"Am I the only one working here today?" she muttered to herself. She glanced around, re-read another e-mail sitting in her draft folder and, with a second look around her, pressed 'send'. "Time for a cigarette break."

She took the stairs all the way; in her mind, it atoned for the poison she was about to put into her lungs. Kerri nodded to Damian, the young guy who'd just started his shift on security - much cuter than Vic the Prick –

and, when the automatic doors slid open with a whisper, she stepped out into the bright spring sunshine.

**

The Rat leant against the corroded iron railings of a boarded-up school. Across the wide piazza, it watched the to-and-fro of the city's largest employer. A caravan of distribution vehicles trundled up a delivery road, mail vans came and went, staff mingled around the entrance like bees round their queen.

If it was to go public, this was the place. The Rat would be as meticulous as ever; introduce itself insidiously and, like dry rot, spread and grow until the entire world knew of its presence.

The Rat may even find a victim here. Plenty to choose from. Tarts in short skirts, others full of hubris, some foul-mouthed. It mattered not; a world of prey awaited. The Rat pushed itself away from the railings and walked across the road.

EcoHug should feel honoured. It was the place where humanity would first learn of The Rat.

**

Melissa Beecham held open her office door and ushered Patsy through it.

"Now you've had a chance to think about everything I've said, how do you feel about Peterborough?"

"Miss Beecham, I'm flattered you think I'm up to the challenge. I really am. But nothing's changed. The circumstances aren't right. The timing's not right."

Beecham shook her head. "I'm sorry you feel that way. And, I must be honest, I'm disappointed in you. Is there anything I can do to make you change your mind?"

Patsy almost said no there-and-then. He thought he should at least pretend to consider the offer. He hesitated for a moment, then said what he knew he would say. "I've too much on. Here, at work. And at home. It just wouldn't be possible. Give it to some thrusting young buck. My time's gone." A thought hit him. "What about Kerri Duncan? Have you thought about her?"

"It's not a job for a woman. Ok. I get what you say about home. But work? Prove it to me. There," she pointed to her desk. "Log yourself onto my PC. Show me your diary for the next three weeks."

"Miss Beecham…"

"Do it. NOW."

Patsy slipped his smartcard into the receptacle with his right hand. The CEO turned her back on him whilst he typed in his password. She stood in front of the EcoHug logo, saw the UK held in the green arms, and felt a pang of envy.

She heard a brief "What the hell?" from Patsy before pandemonium behind her dragged her back to reality from the comfort of the logo's arms. Melissa's chair was propelled across the room. Patsy cowered on the floor, arms wrapped around his head. "Noooo!" He scrabbled away from the PC as if it were a demon.

"Patsy, what the devil…?"

Zoe burst in. "Miss Beecham. Is everything ok?"

"Does it look ok, Zoe? Help me here, will you? Patsy, what's happened?"

Patsy didn't speak. He couldn't. Instead, he pointed a trembling finger in the direction of Beecham's computer. While Zoe comforted the stricken MaGill, Melissa moved closer to the screen.

'I have her.
I will kill her.
You think I won't?
I've killed before.
I kill now.
I will kill again.
You won't find her.
You won't tell anyone.
Why won't you tell anyone?
Because I know who you are.
I know where you are.
I know what you do.
In your worst nightmares you could never guess the things I do.

'I think we are in rats' alley
Where the dead men lost their bones'

Beneath the text lay a grainy thumbnail image lifted from the stills of an old movie. It showed a shallow grave within which lay the barely-covered outline of a body.

**

Melissa straightened. Clutched her desk for support, closed her eyes and breathed deeply.

Patsy lay on the floor like a crushed orchid, his head buried in Zoe's breasts though they barely muffled his sobs.

"Right. Right. Let's think. Patsy – listen to me. Listen to me, ok?" Melissa knelt beside him, laid a hand on his arm. "Whatever this is, whoever this is. It's a prank, yeah?"

Patsy shook his head. Snot and tears and spittle smeared Zoe's sweater.

"Patsy. Please. Calm down." She spoke calmly now, in control, thinking logically. "Think about it. You're not married, are you? You haven't a partner, so far as I know. I believe your parents are dead. Who can he have? It's a prank. A sick joke. And the picture: don't worry about it. It's just some old B-movie poster."

"It's my sister," Patsy wailed. "He's got my sister. That's why I can't do Peterborough. She lives with me. I'm her carer."

Zoe and Melissa looked at each other.

Melissa thought for a moment. "Call her."

"What?"

"Call your sister. She'll answer. I know she will. Then, you'll know it's a prank."

Patsy extricated himself from Zoe's cleavage. He pulled out his phone. Dropped it. Fumbled with the menu. Handed it to Zoe. "You do it. Speed dial number one."

Zoe obliged and handed the phone to Patsy as soon as it began to ring out.

And ring.

And ring.

Melissa swallowed. Zoe held her breath. Patsy did both.

The phone rang some more.

Melissa watched as Patsy's head slumped. He moved the phone down from his ear.

Then snapped it back again.

"Thank God. Thank God. Oh, thank God. Are you ok? You sure? No-one's…no-one's been, have they? Good. Good. No, I'm fine. Honest, I am. Now. I'll see you later. Love you."

He terminated the call and all three wept and laughed and hugged.

Melissa was first to break free. She pulled a bottle from her desk drawer, offered it to Patsy. He shook his head. She swigged a large mouthful before turning her gaze towards her PC.

"Patsy?"

"Hmm?"

"Come here a moment, will you?"

When he joined her, she pointed out the e-mail address. "Know who that is?"

Patsy wiped away tears with the back of his hand. Declined the gin once more. "No. I've no idea."

"Who would do this to you?"

His first thought was Saul. Kerri saying how he'd changed. What were the words she'd used? 'More vitriolic'. "I honestly don't know." He didn't. But he knew it wouldn't be Saul.

He looked at the message again. He pointed at the last sentence. "What's all this about? The rats' alley business?"

Without missing a beat, Melissa replied, "The Wasteland."

"Come again?"

"It's a quote. TS Eliot. From The Wasteland. Or, more accurately, A Game of Chess. Some think it's a reference to the trenches of World War One."

Patsy gave her a curious look.

"I told you I didn't major in science, didn't I?"

He nearly smiled.

"Right, Mr MaGill. I think it's time you got yourself home, don't you? I'm sure you'll be pleased to see your sister. And don't even think about coming in tomorrow. Or even on Wednesday, if you're not up to it."

He did smile, this time. "Thank you, Miss Beecham."

"Melissa, please."

"Thanks, Melissa."

"Oh, and Patsy?"

"Yes?"

"The Peterborough offer's still there."

They both knew she didn't mean it.

**

It was good to get home early. 'That,' he thought, 'Was quite a day'.

Drained, emotional and tired, Patsy climbed the stairs to the terraced house. As he stepped inside, he raised his voice. "Early finish for me today. It's good to be back."

He pulled the bright orange door shut behind him.

DAY NINE

The car roamed the pre-dawn streets. Its driver had slept well. Not long, but well. The mission had started, the road to fame laid with secure foundations. The Rat only needed patience. Soon, once it knew who could be trusted, it could leak news of its gifts more widely. But, for now, it needed to keep up its work.

The car drove past the dimly-lit brewery, shadows everywhere, the omnipresent tinkle of glass from the bottling plant sufficient to drown out screams. It made a mental note of the spot. The site had potential.

The vehicle turned left, almost collided with a near-silent milk float. Milk floats meant houses meant people meant streetlights. No good. And yet…

The road sloped right to left. Access to the lower dwellings came via a sloped pathway, the upper houses required a climb of five or six steps. The Rat looked up as it steered along. The houses were Regency, it surmised. Tall terraced buildings, much larger inside than appeared out.

Midway down the terrace The Rat came to a Doric arch, its centre-stone smoothed with age where a carved date once stood. Beneath the arch ran an alley to an allotment plot to the rear.

Vandals had smashed the streetlights. It was a nice, dark alley.

The Rat smirked. Its car picked up speed and shot past a bright orange door.

**

"He's not coming in, is he?"
"Doesn't look like it."
"Bugger."
Saul sat at his desk, tall green felt hat atop his head, chin festooned with

red woollen beard complete with clay pipe. He pulled off the hat and shook out his hair. "Never mind. I'll save this for another day."

Kerri smiled. "I don't know how he puts up with you, I really don't."

"You make it sound like we're married." Saul's phone rang.

"Saved by the bell," she said.

"Saul Benton". She saw his face screw up. "What, now? This minute? Ok. Give me ten." He harrumphed as he replaced the receiver.

"What's up?"

"Melissa Beecham wants to see me. I reckon she thinks I'm at her beck-and-call."

"Married to her now, as well?"

"Careful. If I'd said that…" He stood to leave.

"Saul?"

"Yeah?"

"You might want to take off the beard."

**

Beecham wore a crisp black suit over a white blouse. She'd carefully arranged her hair so it rested on her shoulders. It shone with a recently-brushed lustre. She smiled the smile of an assassin. "Take a seat, Saul."

Saul regarded the CEO with suspicion. She'd heightened her chair so she sat taller than he; organised the clutter on her desk in a way that shouted controlled importance. She sat looking at him for a full minute. Just as he began to feel uncomfortable, she spoke.

"How would you feel about taking on the Peterborough challenge?"

It was his turn to dish out the silent treatment. At length, he answered with a question. "Why the change of heart?"

"Because I… we…need to move quickly on this."

"I see. But not so quickly that you couldn't afford to wait a week before asking me."

"Explain." A demand, not a question.

"I was certain you were going to ask me last week, yet you didn't. You expressly told me that I wasn't right for it. You had something else lined up for me. So, why now?"

Melissa sat upright. Drummed her fingers on her desk. "I want to show you something." She flicked a switch and a projector screen rolled down from the ceiling. Pressed another button and an image appeared, a graph displaying a green line in a gradual upward arc. "This," she said, "Is the EcoHug sales figures."

Another click and a yellow line overlay the graph. It showed a slight rise across the twelve months-worth of data displayed but, overall, it remained steady. "And this one, our budget and overheads. Salary costs, outlay on maintenance for our older sites, rental on our newer properties such as this office…"

"I know what overheads are."

She gave him a cold look. "Finally, this shows our profit margins." Another click. A red line appeared over two-thirds of the graph, rising exponentially with the sales line.

"I don't see the point of this, Miss Beecham. Why the economics lesson? We're here to talk about relocating the Peterborough plant."

Melissa threw her hands up. "Eureka! That's exactly the point, Saul." He didn't like the way she emphasised 'exactly'. A final click of the button. The red line picked up where it left off – except it plummeted downwards, over a cliff and off the scale.

Saul let out a low whistle. "That doesn't make any sense. Sales increase plus steady overheads equals healthy profit".

"Correct. Except it doesn't, does it?"

"It has to, Miss Beecham. The figures must be wrong."

She let out a chuckle laden with irony. "They're not. So, onto Peterborough." The graph disappeared from the screen to be replaced by the EcoHug logo. "This is the location of our plants." The map of the UK illuminated with green lights, twelve of them. "Are you watching, Saul?"

He rolled his eyes. "I'm watching, Miss." His turn for irony.

The CEO clicked again. One-by-one, five lights turned red, including one mid-way between Birmingham and Norwich. Peterborough.

"We're not relocating our Peterborough plant. We're closing it."

Saul sat still as a tombstone. "None of this makes any sense."

"That's what I thought."

"Is that all you've got? Your company's going down the toilet and you've no grand plan? That's not the Melissa Beecham I know."

She looked at him with pursed lips. "Oh, I'm doing something about it, don't worry about that." She considered for a moment then said softly, "Can I trust you?"

"Of course you can."

"Then come with me. But, take your shoes off."

"What?"

"I know. But humour me. Take off your shoes."

**

Kerri Duncan stretched. She wasn't tired, just bored. She had plenty work to get on with, but it was in the quiet moments she realised how dull and routine her job was. And this certainly was a quiet moment. Patsy and Saul may squabble like an old couple but it was good entertainment, even if one of them did overstep the mark from time to time.

Kerri checked her watch. Saul had been with Beecham for ages. There'd been no word from Patsy. All she had to tune into was the background babble of vacuous office-girl chatter.

She turned her attention to the view but was rewarded with grey skies, grey buildings, grey people. She needed a break. Kerri left the office floor-plate, for once pleased she was a smoker. Smokers can take breaks whenever they wanted.

On the ground floor, she nodded to the bald man on security and rummaged in her bag for her cigarettes with the uncomfortable feeling the security officer's eyes drilled into her back.

**

"It's like a Pharaoh's tomb down here." Saul didn't know why, but the dark emptiness compelled him to whisper.

Melissa led the way. "I know. But he likes it this way."

The curious look she received drew no response. She stopped outside a door. Put her ear to it. Held a finger to her lips. She eased the door open. No light escaped. She pushed it a little more.

The man inside immediately snapped shut a laptop and spun to face them, eyes cast to the floor.

Cyrus Dilley.

Dilley sat amidst a horse-shoe workstation surrounded by PC screens and a rack of keyboards as if he were Rick Wakeman in his pomp.

"Relax, Cyrus. It's us."

The IT guru pointed his head in the direction of Benton. "I don't think he should be here."

"Don't worry. We can trust him."

"We can't trust anyone."

"Look," said Saul. "Will someone tell me what the hell is going on here?"

Beecham looked for somewhere to sit. There wasn't so she leant against the wall. "You said it yourself. 'The figures don't make any sense'. Yet, both Mashcombe-Fuller and Pole Star Chemicals have just announced soaring pre-tax profits to the City. With less share of the market and much greater import / export levies."

Saul sucked in air. "How'd they manage it?"

"Well, they're either much smarter than us, or there's skulduggery at play.

And that's what Mr Dilley is here to find out, isn't it, Cyrus?"

Cyrus gave a simple nod of the head.

"How?"

Melissa snickered. "Let's just say he's asking a few questions."

"Of?"

"Their systems. Cyrus is checking how robust they are."

Recognition blossomed. "You mean he's hacking, don't you?"

"Congratulations, Mr Benton. Go to the top of the class."

Cyrus shut down the systems one-by-one. "But it's slow work. I can only go undetected for short periods at a time. Ten minutes, max. And it requires intense concentration. With no interruptions." His eyes hardened as he looked in their direction. He didn't need eye contact to get the message over.

Melissa held up her Jimmy Choo's "Hence the hush."

Saul nodded. "I had no idea all this kit was down here."

Cyrus opened his mouth to speak but Melissa shushed him. "I'm sure you want to give Mr Benton chapter and verse but I know once you start you'll never stop. Besides, we need you to give it another burst." She patted the lap-top.

"I don't use this. I've got more than enough gear here without needing a laptop."

Saul thought he saw a nerve in Dilley's cheek twitch but it was impossible to be sure. He had such a poker face.

**

The clock showed five-thirty. He'd been with Melissa all day. "Miss Beecham, I'm really sorry. I need to get home. See how Steph is."

"Saul, I have to move on this one. Cyrus is making progress but its slow progress. Regardless of the figures, of what Cyrus might uncover, the Peterborough plant isn't productive. It's been our least viable plant for some time now. It can't be sustained. We need to close it. So, are you with me?"

She fixed him with baby-blue eyes but he didn't melt. "I've got Steph to consider."

She pulled a not-another-one expression. "Sleep on it. But I need an answer in the morning."

"You sound like Meat Loaf."

Melissa twisted her face. "I can't give you a moment more."

"Ok. It's a deal," he said. "Now, may I phone a cab? The X-Trail's in for a service. Well, if I'm being honest, it's in for a deep valet. You wouldn't believe the crap I've had in the trunk lately." After a beat he added, "Doing up a nursery for little Roland. Been taking stuff to the household waste centre."

"Listen, I'm about done here myself. Can I give you a lift?"

"That'll be great, if you're sure. I mean, for all you know, I could be a serial killer."

Melissa laughed. "I doubt it, somehow. After all, the odds of two of them being together in the same room must be astronomical."

She reached beneath her desk. "Here, you'll need this." She flung something in his direction. He caught it with the reflexes of a slip fielder. In his hands, he held a shiny black motor-cycle helmet.

"You're full of surprises."

**

Suki Chan was late.

The banquet at Kyoto's had been delectable but the free-flowing Kissui took its toll. She'd lost track of time and now she'd lost her bearings. The last train left in five minutes and she was the wrong side of the tracks. In more ways than one.

The faster she moved, the more her head swam. She checked her watch one more time, the face way too large for her tiny wrist. It showed 11.43. She upped her pace. The high-pitched screech of metal-on-metal, like the agonised roar of a wounded beast, signalled the approach of her train.
Suki hurried under the railway arch.

The thrum of the train's wheels reverberated through her, matching the pounding of her heart beat-for-beat. Suki heard something else. Footsteps. Behind her. Another late passenger. No comfort to her.

Red-hot pain seared through her head as something caught her hair. Her head jerked backwards, lifting her off her feet at the same time as a hand clamped over her mouth.

DAY TEN

Patsy MaGill woke to undraped windows and a view smothered by a heavy blanket of cloud. Anger welled within him, an emotion he rarely experienced. How dare someone target him, threaten his beloved sister. He felt uncomfortable in his anger. He shifted focus to WHY they would do it. Why him? What had he done? Who had he upset? Patsy couldn't shake the thoughts from his head. He rose early with the intention of going to work but he knew he wasn't ready. Not yet.

Meanwhile, Saul Benton woke to an empty bed. No sign of Steph alongside him. He was angry, too. Angry his wife shunned him. Angry Melissa Beecham had toyed with him over the Peterborough thing. Angry she'd misled him. Most of all, he was angry he couldn't remember.

In the room below, Steph Benton sat on the recliner. She hadn't slept. Roland had converted several penalties from the twenty-two metre line inside her womb overnight, and Saul was being, well, Saul. Steph was annoyed; furious she couldn't find the fragments of her life hidden behind the cushions, no matter how much she searched.

Cyrus Dilley sat at his horse-shoe workstation. He'd been there all night. Well, almost all night. He wasn't happy. He did his best work alone. Beecham knew that, yet now it looked like she intended bringing someone else in. This wasn't why she'd recruited him. He wouldn't let her get away with it. This was his project and no-one – not even a man; let alone a man like Saul Benton – was going to stop him.

Vic Pritchard rarely took a day off. The one day he had something planned, he'd received an overnight call to say Damian Dalglish had taken ill. Could he cover? Typical. True, the agency had offered to send someone else, but they'd suggested Marian Anderson. A woman. A woman couldn't be trusted to protect EcoHug. It was a man's job. No, he'd said, he'd cancel his leave.

Melissa Beecham woke in a bad mood. She half-expected Benton would turn down the Peterborough project this morning. Typical. Not only had she taken him into her confidence, she'd also brought him up to speed with the company's fortunes. And briefed him on Dilley's true purpose. How dare he? At least, she comforted herself, he hadn't suggested she offer the role to a woman. Unlike Patsy MaGill.

Kerri Duncan set off for the office. She felt in her bones that Patsy would be absent again. As for Saul, he'd surely have bigger fish to fry after his all-day session with Beecham. Another day of the interminable dross churned out by office-junior Denise and her friends was just what she didn't need, today of all days.

Yes, The Rat was angry, all right. Angry that Suki Chan would have to wait. But she'd pay for it tonight. Boy, would she pay for it? The Rat toyed with something at its side, licking its lips in anticipation.

**

Outside, clouds had consumed the earth. It wasn't raining, exactly, yet the air was filled with moisture. She dripped as if melting. The doors swished open and she entered another world.
Hemispherical onyx statues stood around a shallow water feature. Open spaces, soft furnishings and low-level lighting completed the feng shui feel while soft mood muzak filtered from speakers concealed within the high ceiling.
So, this is where he worked.
Steph Benton looked around in awe as a puddle formed at her feet. She knew he worked on the ninth floor. She took off in the direction of the twin elevators situated behind a low-level desk.
"Pass," said a man behind the desk.
"I don't work here."
"Then you can't come in." He turned a leaf of the Times Literary Supplement.
"My husband work's here."

"Congratulations."

Steph swallowed. "Can I see him?"

"Depends."

"Look, I'm in no mood for games. Can I see my husband? Please."

"You're married?"

"I am. For now, anyway."

"How do I know you're married? You're not wearing a ring."

How did he know her wedding band no longer fitted? She hadn't seen the man look up from his magazine. She unzipped her coat to reveal her bump.

Vic the Prick snorted. "Means nothing these days. You could be any trollop."

Steph opened her mouth to protest as the elevator doors opened. A man stepped out. "He's not wearing a pass." She pointed in the man's direction. "That's discrimination."

The man in the elevator opened and closed his fingers. He looked anywhere but at the security guy or Steph as he said, "I don't need one."

Vic recognised the soft voice behind him. "True. He's head of IT. Morning, Mr Dilley."

Steph looked the man up-and-down. "Him? Oh, yeah: and I'm Joan of Arc. Come on, I'm in no mood for this. Let me in."

"You're in no mood? It's supposed to be my day off. How do you think I feel?"

The man with streaky-grey hair said, "I'll be back in twenty minutes. You will let me in, Mr Pritchard, won't you?" He added pointedly, "Without a pass, that is."

"Sure thing, Mr Dilley."

Vic stared at Steph until she averted her eyes. "Name?" he barked.

"Mine or my husband's?"

"Both."

The elevator doors opened again. A power-dressed dark haired woman stepped out. "Victor, I'm due an early-morning meeting which I have to delay. I've left a message but in case he goes straight to my room, could you keep an eye out for Saul Benton arriving? Let him know I'll be in touch very soon."

The woman looked at Steph and offered a simper of a smile. It wasn't returned.

"Who was that?" Steph asked.

"Our CEO, Miss Beecham."

Steph watched the woman's back as she unfolded her umbrella and stepped into the drizzle.

Victor coughed to get her attention. "Name?"

"Steph Benton. Here to see Saul Benton." She looked at her watch. "And I don't know why he isn't here yet."

Vic squinted at her suspiciously. "Popular, isn't he?"

Steph watched a dark-haired woman duck into a cab. "With some people, yes."

**

Pastries and baguettes, muffins and cookies stared out from a glass display cabinet like wide-eyed puppies seeking a new home. A line of customers pointed at them and licked their lips in anticipation.

At a corner table, a man sat alone. Watching.

The line crawled forward. Behind the counter, a well-oiled engine kicked into gear. One girl took orders; the guy next to her populated a tray with cups and tail-wagging savouries. To his left, a girl took payment while the final two baristas stood next to a silver machine that gurgled and hissed and steamed like a beast from ancient mythology.

The man in the corner wondered why no-one else saw a car assembly line in action, the customers vehicles under construction. He was so engrossed he didn't notice someone occupy the chair next to him.

"I hope this is good, Mr Dilley."

"It's not. It's not good at all."

Melissa Beecham sighed. "And?"

"I think Pole Star may be onto us."

She let out a low groan and a whistle simultaneously, the sound of a balloon deflating. "I thought you knew how to avoid detection."

He drummed a beat on the table while his eyes never left his espresso. "Nothing's fool-proof, and I'm still not certain, but a trojan entered my system when I hooked up to the Pole Star mainframe. I set things up so it should be a one-way stream but something's entered, all the same."

"Jesus Christ. So, we're rumbled."

"That depends. I was on-line when the trojan entered and I managed to quarantine it immediately. They won't necessarily know it's us but Pole Star, or whoever it is, will be alerted to the fact someone's tried to hack in."

Melissa closed her eyes. "I pray to God they don't know it's us. I hope you're right."

"There is a positive, though."

She met his eyes, only for Cyrus to glance away. "Which is?"

"Two positives, actually. One: I can work on the trojan undetected in quarantine. See if I can discover anything from it."

Melissa nodded. "You said there were two positives."

Cyrus locked eyes with her. "It means they've got something to hide."

**

An instrumental version of Fire and Rain greeted Saul as he stepped onto the slick tiles inside EcoHug's HQ. He shook himself out like a sodden Retriever fresh from the canal and mused on the capriciousness of a British springtime.

He was halfway towards the elevator when Vic intercepted him. "A word to the wise. Your missus is here. I've directed her to the Reception Lounge."

"Steph's here? What does she want?" Vic shrugged but the face he pulled told all. Saul glanced at his watch. "She'll have to wait. Got an appointment with the CEO."

Vic gurned again, this one full of sympathy. "Sorry, Mr Benton, Miss Beecham's had to pop out. Told me she'd…"

"We need to talk, Saul. Not in the lounge; it's too busy."

Confused and concerned, he left Vic and led his wife to a quiet spot in the lobby. He helped lower her onto a seat. "Is everything all right? With the baby?"

"Which of those questions do you want me to answer first?" Her response was curt, no warmth in her voice. Without waiting for a reply, she steamrollered on. "The baby's fine." Saul visibly relaxed. "But, no: everything's not 'all right'. Far from it."

Saul scratched his head. He opened his mouth to speak, but Steph carried on, as if she'd rehearsed what she was about to say and nothing was going to interrupt her. "It was only Saturday when you promised you'd change. You'd be with me, you said. Mend your ways. Well, since you made that promise, things have got worse, not better. You've hardly been home, have you? You've been up Mother's Mound walking, on the drink with Patsy, getting so drunk it took you hours to get home."

"Steph…" She raised her hand. The gesture screamed 'talk to this'. He shut up.

"But last night just about took the biscuit. Good God, man, you didn't even realise I wasn't in bed with you. I could've had Roland on the bathroom floor for all you care and…"

Saul stood. "Stop! I've had enough of this. You come to my workplace to tell me this? Buzzing in my ear like an irritating fly that goes on, and on, and on again. You're an embarrassment, don't you know. You're making a fool of yourself. No wonder you didn't want this conversation in the lounge.

Folk would call the funny farm."

"And speaking of work, you should have been here ages ago. Where were you?"

"Picking my car up from the garage, woman".

The doors slid open. A draft of cold air washed over them like the ghost of their marriage. The couple who came in from the downpour looked over at the raised voices. A man in scruffy cargo jeans turned his head away. The woman, more curious, took a longer look. Steph glared back. The woman glanced between Saul and Steph and ushered Cyrus behind the security barrier.

"Now look what you've done," Saul hissed. "I have an important meeting with her. Important to our future. Mine, yours, and Roland's. She's the CEO, for God's sake."

Melissa snapped a laugh laden with sarcasm. "She's also the woman who brought you home yesterday. On the back of her bike. She dropped you out of sight behind the Leylandii. Where you thought I couldn't see you. But you forgot about the CCTV. It was her, wasn't it?" The question was rhetorical. Tears spilled from her eyes. "I saw you, Saul. The pair of you. Together."

Saul's mouth lolled open like a goldfish. No words came.

"I've had it. I'm leaving you. I'm going to stay with my mother. When you get home tonight, IF you ever get home tonight, I'll be long gone." She caressed her belly. "We both will."

**

In a dark confined cupboard of an office, the mainframe systems sat dormant. Cyrus Dilley viewed the Pole Star revelation as a challenge; not an insurmountable challenge to his intellect but a test nonetheless.

In the meantime, he'd research and plan other tasks. He logged onto the laptop. The fingers of his left hand danced a merry jig while he fathomed the way forward. The words of his old university lecturer came back to him. 'Ignore those people who say we learn from history,' she'd told him many years ago. 'When it comes to technology, history is bunk - because there isn't any history. Nor is there a present. There's only the future.'

Just as she was wrong about so many things, she was wrong about that, too. After all, where did the term 'trojan' come from if not history itself? Certain in his own mind, Cyrus entered the website.

Kerri Duncan also surfed the web although she did focus on the future, not the past. She didn't know what Melissa and Saul were working on, but she was sure it wouldn't include her. Despite the last couple of weeks, she enjoyed working with Saul. His irreverent and unconventional approach brightened the day, something the last few days sadly lacked. If he was moving on, then so must she.

The job search website held nothing for her. She resigned herself to staying put. For now. At least Patsy would still be there. She worried about Patsy. It was unlike him not to be in touch.

A thought hit her. It stopped her in her tracks. She feared his tumour had returned. Kerri picked up her phone before realising she hadn't his new number.

'It'll just be a spring cold,' she told herself, and resumed her job search.

**

The Rat entered a zen-like state. Inhaled to the count of three, held it for three beats, and exhaled for three seconds. It repeated the act three times. By the time the exercise was over, The Rat was in another place. An empty concrete space on The Gallows estate where a waif-like Oriental girl waited.

Something stirred within The Rat; something more than excitement. Something urgent and primordial. The Rat had no further need for the anatomical research papers, the medical dictionaries, or the modes of practice. Its research was complete.

A grin, a leer, spread over The Rat's features.

This was destiny. This was redemption. This was nirvana.

**

Zoe buzzed Saul through.

"Peterborough. Count me in. When do I start?" No preamble. He meant business.

Melissa disguised a smile of satisfaction and pretended to continue studying the portfolio in front of her. She shifted in her seat. Crossed her legs. "Good." She still hadn't raised her head from the papers.

"I have some questions first."

Dynamic. To the point. Assertive. Melissa liked all those things. "Fire away." She motioned him to take a seat. He declined, preferred to pace back and forth. Melissa stood in response.

"Firstly," he said. "Let's talk about a post-delivery bonus." She made a note. "Secondly, I want to know why you delayed asking me. I hope I'm not second choice." He made a point of holding eye-contact. She didn't look away so he continued.

"Thirdly, I want to know about London."

She lowered an eyelid in puzzlement, let out air, and then beamed a disarming smile. "You've got yourself a deal, Mr Benton. Almost. Now, sit. Please." The last word didn't hide the fact it was a command. "But, first, you answer me something."

Her voice changed. "What the bloody hell was going on in the lobby?"

At that, Saul did sit. "Sorry. She shouldn't have brought a domestic to my workplace. I've got a lot going on at home but I assure you it won't interfere with my work. It can't when I'm in Peterborough. I apologise. She shouldn't have come here."

"'She' being who, exactly?"

"Steph. My wife. Or, at least, the most recent ex-Mrs Benton." He surprised himself at the tone of sadness in his voice. Fought to regain control of the discussion. "You were about to answer my questions."

Melissa moved closer to him on the office sofa. She crossed her legs. His nostrils flared involuntarily at the scent of her perfume. He edged away before making a conscious effort to relax his body language. Saul tried a miserable attempt at humour. "Are you flirting with me?" He gave an embarrassed smile. Why the hell had he said that?

Melissa Beecham let out a sharp laugh. "Saul, believe me, you'd know if I was flirting. THIS is flirting." She'd lowered her voice to a husky whisper, tilted her head down so she stared up at him with doe-eyes. She threw him her best pout, dangled a shoe off one foot and, while one hand twisted a strand of hair, the other lay on his thigh, fingers upward.

Abruptly, she stood. Walked to the window. Her normal voice returned. "Now, where were we?"

Saul cleared his throat. "We were a couple of inches away from needing VAR, that's where we were."

She ignored him. "Oh yes. Your questions. I have to tell you, yes – you are second choice."

A scowl crossed his face. "And who, may I ask, was first choice?"

"Patsy MaGill."

The scowl turned to incredulity. "Patsy?"

"Yes. Patsy MaGill. Your mentor. But he turned it down."

Incredulity turned to concern. "You haven't suspended him for refusing, have you? Is that why he's gone AWOL?"

She gave a tell-tale glance towards the PC on her desk. "I can't tell you why Saul's not with us but he's not AWOL and his absence isn't related to Peterborough, I assure you."

Saul ran a hand down his face. He was second choice, after all. But, with Steph gone, did it really matter? He pressed on. "My bonus?"

"No bonus." She held up a hand to quell his protest. "But a promotion. Nicholas Irvine is taking early retirement. I'd like you to succeed him as one of my Assistant Director's. However, that depends on two things."

He motioned for her to continue.

"To begin with, it's dependent upon you making sufficient efficiencies to justify your salary. Peterborough must be mothballed, and without any bad publicity. EcoHug's in enough strife without local MPs on our case, or striking workers on TV."

Saul tilted his head in agreement. Melissa continued. "On top of that, I need you to park the fly-by-night Saul. No jokes, no off-the-cuff remarks, just total professionalism. Be the Saul Benton I first saw in London."

Saul tried to retain a poker face. He doubted it worked. AD. A double-promotion. Wow! But one more question remained unanswered. And she had provided him with the get-in. "Melissa, do you remember London?" She nodded, he hesitated. "The day Hugh cried off and I presented on his behalf. I got rat-assed that night, drunk as a skunk with relief I'd got through it and delight at the audience's response."

He paused. Wondered how to broach the subject. He took a deep breath and dove straight in. "In the morning, when I woke up, I was in your room. You weren't there. You'd already left to travel to Birmingham. It's the one thing that's preyed on my mind ever since. I wish I could remember without asking, but I can't. I need to know. For Steph's sake – wherever she might be right now – I need to know, Melissa. Did we…you know?"

"Are you taking the Peterborough project?"

"Yes, I am. Now, answer the question. Please. It's haunted me for months. I have to know."

"I'm sorry, Saul. I can't tell you. It's commercial-in-confidence."

Melissa Beecham's face was as enigmatic as the Mona Lisa.

Alley Rat

DAY ELEVEN

'I can feel it coming in the air tonight, oh Lord'

The drum beat rumbled within the pitch-dark concrete shell of a building. A naked Suki Chan shuddered at the sound as it echoed to fade.

'And I've been waiting for this moment for all of my life, oh Lord'

Despite her poor grasp of English, the slip of a girl didn't need the lyrics translated. Western music was familiar throughout her Japanese mother's homeland, even if it hadn't reached the hinterland of her father's native China.

'Well I remember. Don't worry, how could I ever forget?'

Through her tears, Suki saw her parents, thousands of miles away. Memories came; memories of her father desperate to see his little girl learn Western-ways, arguing with his wife who insisted Japan presented her with more opportunities, begging him not to send her baby girl abroad.

'It's the first time, the last time, we ever met'

The room flooded with light. Cockroaches scuttled in all directions, seeking refuge beneath the floor and in wall cavities. The room fell silent.
Suki blinked to absorb the brightness. An immature twenty-four-year-old, in the vast chamber she could have passed for fourteen. She shied from her nakedness, unable to hide it.

Someone sat watching her.

Some thing.

The Rat.

It ogled her with barely concealed contempt. Then, it sneered. This one would be so very different, The Rat thought. So much more enjoyable.

The Rat looked at the tool in its hand. It had moulded it for some time. An implement from ancient history. The Rat closed its eyes and luxuriated in the stench of the girl's whimpering fear.

She rattled her chains. Not in an escape attempt. The girl shook and trembled in abject terror. The convulsions ran through her and up her restraining shackles.

The Rat moved towards the child-woman. Someone so young, so tender, should never be allowed out so late. Unless, of course, she, too, was as nefarious as the addict and the whore. The Rat rotated the tool in its hand, its eyes caressing it.

Suki also watched the object in her captor's hands. She didn't know what it was. It resembled a pair of tongs, an implement you'd use to remove ice-cubes from a bucket. But three times the size. Cast iron.

With ends chamfered into vicious claws.

Suki couldn't drag her eyes from it. Unintelligible words flowed from her, a tsunami of pleas The Rat would never listen to even if it could understand. A spider crawled the length of the girl's leg, crossed her hairless belly and felt its way upwards towards her small breasts.

"A sign." The Rat's voice was hushed, flat, as it watched the arachnid explore the girl's body. Suki didn't seem to notice. Her captor's voice commanded all her attention.

The Rat held up the implement. "This, my little China girl, is also called a Spider. Very apt, don't you think?"

The girl didn't understand a word. She just kept alternating her wide-eyed glare between The Rat and the tool.

"Answer me!" The metal Spider rushed towards the girl's face. She jerked her head sideways as the spiked edge ripped through her cheek. A splash of crimson spattered the wall, adorned the graffiti on it. The cuffs dug into her wrists as her hands tried to protect her face.

Her captor's voice raised an octave. "Are those tears? Not so inscrutable now, are we?" The Rat brought the weapon alongside the creature nestling between the girl's breasts. Blood dripped from the tool onto her almost translucent skin.

"Let me tell you what this is." He pointed a claw at the girl's eyes. She quaked and tried to pull away from it. "It seems it's something that was used during the Spanish Inquisition. Do you know what the Spanish Inquisition is?"

No answer other than snivelling wails.

"Never mind, my child. It's not important. What is important to you is its other name." The Rat rolled the Spider against the girl's torso.

"The Spider was also known as the Breast Ripper."

With speed that rendered the movement a blur, the hook skewered the girl's breast. The Rat twisted and gouged and hauled on the Spider, digging deeper into the flesh, deep towards Suki's chest cavity.

The girl's falsetto screams echoed around the concrete cavern. The Rat hauled the Spider from the girl's chest, drawing with it swathes of flesh, muscle and tissue, and clamped it on her tongue. The fleshy appendage slithered out of Suki's mouth, slid onto her collar bone, and drifted away on a crimson river. Suki screamed no more.

The Rat returned the Spider to its rightful place. Blood flowed and congealed from the sinkhole in the poor girl's chest. The Spider clamped down inside the maw, twisting severed blood vessels, dragging out the last musculature.

Suki Chan prayed for death to come. It didn't. Her tormentor wasn't finished.

The hook plunged into her remaining breast. The tongs squeezed together. The Rat released them and squeezed once more. It writhed at her tissue like a crocodile performing the death roll. Blood soaked The Rat. The more it drenched the killer, the more frantic the Spider's work became; work that lasted another five, long, minutes.

Mercifully, Suki Chan lost consciousness before a cockroach sought safer refuge from the frenzy. It darted inside the dying girl's body.

**

Traffic buzzed around EcoHug plaza like wasps at a picnic. Saul Benton waited for a gap before sprinting across, flight bag a faithful puppy at his heels.

He breathed in the clear April air and entered the building with a spring in his step. Bill Withers greeted him with the chorus to Lovely Day as he flashed his ID at a flustered-looking woman behind the Security Desk. Even Victor Pritchard wasn't there to wreck his mood.

The elevator sailed past the ninth floor. After a quick comb of his hair, he breezed past Zoe into Melissa Beecham's office. The sight of the CEO stopped him in his tracks. Gaunt. Pale-faced. Agitated.

It clearly wasn't a lovely day after all.

"Bad time?" he asked.

She nodded, mouth a thin line.

"Want to tell me about it?"

This time, she shook her head. He didn't know what to say. Settled for "Ok. I just wanted to let you know I'm on the 9.50 to Peterborough. A couple of days reconnaissance mission, then I'll set up camp down there next week."

Melissa remained silent, her pallor whiter still.

The door opened. Zoe spoke in a whisper. "Mr MaGill is here, Miss Beecham. And Mr Dilley's just arrived in the building. I'll send him in directly."

Saul met Patsy with a handshake. "Good to see you again, Patsy." The greeting was restrained. He'd caught the mood. This was no time for frivolity. 'What's up?' he mouthed. Patsy shrugged.

"Patsy," Beecham said, "Sit down, please."

Saul didn't know whether the invitation extended to him but he sat, too.

Patsy spoke. "What's this about, Miss Beecham?" The CEO didn't respond. "I was planning on coming back next week but I can start today if that's the problem."

Beecham's eyes kept flicking to her PC. She withdrew a bottle of gin from her bottom drawer, poured some into a glass but spilled more onto her desk.

Saul and Patsy exchanged glances and raised eyebrows. She didn't notice. Her focus was on her monitor screen.

The office door opened again. Zoe ushered in Cyrus Dilley, his eyes on the EcoHug logo above their heads. His arrival seemed to jerk Beecham back to reality.

"Gentlemen, we have a problem. A big problem."

The men in suits assumed worried expressions. The man in jeans looked as he always did, except the movement of his fingers increased in pace.

"Some of you know some of this. None of you know it all. For Patsy's benefit, EcoHug is in financial trouble. Things aren't as they should be. We suspect one of our competitors – it now seems most likely to be Pole Star – infiltrated our systems and, in some way we don't yet know or understand, affected and adjusted our financial position. And I mean seriously adjusted."

Patsy didn't follow. Not yet. But he knew now was not the time to interject.

"Mr Dilley is working on it. Or I should say 'was'. It's become…" she searched for a word, "Complicated."

Dilley nodded. He opened his mouth to explain further but Melissa hushed him.

"Now, a few days ago, Patsy received a particularly abhorrent e-mail."

Saul looked at his friend, concerned. Patsy looked straight ahead.

"The e-mail," Beecham continued, "Made vile threats against his sister."

Saul was confused. "Sister? I didn't know you…" It was Saul's turn to receive the finger-to-lips treatment. He shut up.

"I must tell you the threats were without substance but, understandably in the circumstances, I granted Patsy some time away." MaGill shifted uncomfortably. "Patsy, when you left, you did so in a hurry. You didn't log out of my PC or remove your smartcard from it."

Patsy didn't know where this was going. Dilley wondered why he was there. And Saul feared Beecham had found something incriminating on Patsy's profile.

While their thoughts followed different paths, Beecham revealed all. "Patsy, this morning, you got another e-mail from the same unknown address. The message was largely the same." She read it aloud.

"I told you The Rat had her.
You didn't believe me.
I didn't say who she was.
This is her.
Nice, isn't she.
I wonder who will be next.
That depends whether you tell anyone.
You won't tell anyone, will you?
Because you know what will happen."

Saul couldn't make sense of any of it but, when Patsy asked, "Is that all? No poem or anything?" he realised it meant something to Patsy.

Saul pulled a face. "Poem?"

Melissa spoke. "There was. In the attachment. This is the attachment."

Melissa sucked air between her teeth. Steeled herself. Looked into the faces of the men. After a moment's hesitation, she clicked on an icon beneath the text and swung her monitor around.

A jpeg revealed itself.

A jpeg of a shredded torso.

**

Patsy and Saul jumped to their feet. Reeled further away from the abomination on the screen.

"What the fuck."

"Jesus Christ."

Cyrus Dilley remained impassive and studied the image. "Fascinating," he said.

Saul came back at him. "Are you for real? 'Fascinating'. Have you heard yourself, Mr Spock? For fuck's sake, look at it, man."

Dilley did look at it. "It's a fake."

"What?" All three of them together.

"It's a fake. It's too neat to be genuine."

Saul snarled at the IT man. "Neat? You seen a lot of these, have you?"

Dilley flicked at his hair. Saul noticed the finger pincer movements slow. "I have, as it happens."

Three faces turned towards him.

"On TV. Holby City. ER, Casualty. Any number of hospital dramas or horror movies. It's an FX model."

The other three looked back at the image. The open chest wall, exposed heart and lungs, empty breast sacks laid over the girl's face. Somehow, knowing it wasn't real made it acceptable to gawp.

Then Dilley spoiled it. "I'd need to do some work on the image to be sure."

Beecham closed the attachment. "That's precisely what you're here for. I also want you to trace the e-mail address. That should be easy, shouldn't it?"

"Depends how clever they are."

Melissa chewed her lip. "Hmmm. Thought it would be straightforward. Ok, this becomes your priority. Leave the other stuff. All of it. Pole Star are onto us anyway."

"We are going to the police with this as well, of course," Saul added.

Melissa walked to the window. Looked over the city, life carrying on for everyone out there. "I've been thinking about that. No, we don't."

"Come on, Melissa. You've got to. We don't know it's a fake."

"I think it probably is, you know. I think it's part of Pole Star's strategy. Not only have they attacked our systems, I suspect this…whatever it is,,, is their work. They're out to discredit us. Bad publicity will kill us. It'll be the end of EcoHug. That's what they want. To hound us out of business. No, we keep things quiet. At least until Cyrus gets us some answers."

Saul nodded. It made sense. Sort of. "We tell the board, though."

Melissa shook her head. "No. Only we know about this. It may be an all-male boardroom but I can't trust them any more than I'd trust a woman over this. I can't be sure they're all with us."

Cyrus spoke. "You mean it's an inside job? You may be right, Miss Beecham. You may well be right."

Melissa walked back to them. "Ok. So, as far as everyone else is concerned, we carry on as normal. Saul to Peterborough, Cyrus to whatever you have to do in your broom cupboard of an office, and Patsy – you go back home." She clapped her hands twice. "Right come on. Off we go."

Cyrus and Saul marched out. Only Patsy remained. "Melissa. You mentioned a poem?"

She nodded. "Ah yes. Eliot again. 'Hysteria.' Here it is. Look." She opened the gruesome image again.

Patsy leaned towards the screen. "Where? I can't see any poem."

She zoomed in. Scrolled up as the image enlarged until the wax model, or whatever it was, dropped off the screen's lower edge. She focused on graffiti scrawled on the blood-stained wall; graffiti newer and bolder than the rest.

'I decided that if the shaking of her breasts could be stopped,
Some of the fragments of the afternoon might be collected,
And I concentrated my attention with careful subtlety to this end.'

**

He'd missed the 9.50 and the 10.15, whilst the 10.50 was running late. Rather than wait, he'd made the decision to squeeze onto a two-carriage bone-shaker which hit every signal at red and chose to stop at each hick village the track dissected.

The train was packed to the rafters. People stood in aisles, shoulder to shoulder, hip-to-hip. The woman alongside Saul had hygiene issues while the man in the aisle seat rested his head against his thigh and snored like a Common Warthog. Not the start he'd planned though it did have its advantages. It took his mind off memories of Steph. More importantly, it diverted his attention from visions of the thing on Melissa Beecham's monitor.

The more Saul thought about it, the surer he became. It wasn't a wax model. Or a dummy. In fact, he knew it wasn't.

When the woman trampled on his toes for the God-knows-how-many'th time, he vowed to get off the train at the next stop.

**

The car sat in a layby on a derelict industrial estate like a rowing boat adrift in an ocean.

The driver took in the surroundings. Breeze-block and concrete buildings, their windows long-since vandalised so they stood like empty eye-sockets against grey bone, lined the arrow-straight road. Where areas of greenery once brightened the surroundings, ugly weeds replaced finely-pruned topiary. Moss ran amok over neglected footpaths.

Although the new moon, a thin gash in a coal black canvas, shed insufficient light to cast shadow, the driver felt naked and exposed. The engine fired up and the vehicle pulled away.

A boarded-up garage slipped by, an abandoned café and disused pre-fabricated buildings followed. When the car arrived outside a larger, hulking construction, it drew to a halt.

The driver glanced at the dashboard clock. It showed 23.52. The vehicle's window opened. A face peered upwards. The lettering on the flank of the building was no more but, in the mind of the car's occupant, it still shone brightly.

'EcoHug.'

Alley Rat

DAY TWELVE

On the stroke of midnight, the car edged towards the alley's mouth. The driver hesitated. It was eerily quiet. Too quiet. Normally, there would be others here. Not many, but some.

The vehicle's headlights dimmed. Its driver fumbled in the glove box until flesh touched leather. The fingers withdrew the item. Opened it. Felt inside. Satisfied there was sufficient within it for the need, the driver tossed the object onto the passenger-side dash. It would be used soon.

As if five red lights turned green, the car entered the alleyway. It was deserted. It shouldn't be like this.

It felt wrong.

The passenger door opened. An attractive woman stepped in. Pretty, dark-haired and shapely. She smiled. Winked. They struck a deal.

Now it felt right. This would be good.

Without warning, a vehicle entered the opposite end of the narrow alley, engine racing, headlights on full-beam. It sped towards the first car, slewed to a halt in front of it blocking the exit.

One car door slammed shut. A shadow dashed across the front of the windscreen. The door opened. A man leaned in. The passenger tossed the leather item to the man who'd opened the door.

The man spoke. "Nice work, Michelle." They exchanged high-fives. He rifled through the object Michelle had passed him until he found the ID he was looking for.

The man turned to the driver. "Section 71 of the Criminal Justice and Police Act 2001 makes it an offence to kerb-crawl with the intent to procure sexual services".

The driver blanched. He knew what was coming. His world collapsed in on him.

The man at the door continued. "I am arresting you under suspicion of committing an offence under the Sexual Offences Act 1985."

The cop put his hand on top of the driver's bald head. It felt clammy. His other hand took the driver by the arm.

"Step out of the car for me, Mr Pritchard."

**

Patsy pressed two fingers against his abdomen and drew them across his stomach. The scar tissue felt rough beneath his finger tips. He manipulated them, kneading his upper stomach. He found nothing else. The constant fear of it coming back haunted him yet each time he examined himself, his worries were assuaged.

Troubled eyes stared back at him from the mirror, forcing him to turn his back on his reflection. All was well. With him, anyway. His attention turned to his sister. Time to find out how she was this sunny spring day.

Across the hallway, the darkness of the room heightened the lilac fragrance in the air. Patsy tip-toed to the window and drew open Laura Ashley curtains, inch-by-inch.

"Shut those curtains," a voice demanded.

He closed them instantly. The room retreated into its shell of lilac and night.

**

Some people light up a room with their presence. A frisson runs through the air like static before a storm. Then there's the other type: the ones who slink in accompanied by the stench of decay. They suck the life out of everything in it.

Sod's law that the man Saul Benton chose to meet on his first day in Peterborough belonged right in the centre of the second category.

The dour Scotsman was an archetypal Trade Union man. Ruddy, vein-splattered complexion, permanent scowl, monosyllabic grunts punctuated by lengthy periods of left-wing diatribe. 'This can only go well,' Saul thought.

"John. Pleased to meet you," Saul lied. "Please, sit down."

The man called John left Saul's hand hanging for a second to give an impression of control before he took it in a vice-like grip. Saul smiled to himself and let John win the 'I've-got-a-bigger-dick-than-you' contest.

"How are things down here?"

"You tell me, bonny lad."

Despite his natural instincts, he kept the smile painted on his face. This was time for him to do what Melissa had demanded of him. Portray a professional image. Win the man's confidence and Saul's hale-fellow-well-met and Jack the Lad personas could emerge later.

"You'll no doubt be wondering why I'm here."

"Aye. But it'll no' be good news, I wager."

Saul turned to the window. Looked out over an area of five football fields covered with brick edifices, tall chimneys and pipes, and metal containers resembling giant moonshine stills. "Impressive facility you've got here." He was mindful not to take ownership. This had to be John's territory, not his or the company's.

John joined him at the window. "It's the men who make it what it is, no' the facility."

"And you've plenty of good men and women here, I bet. Men who've spent many years here."

John answered with a curt nod. "So, what're you here t'do to these 'good men', Mr Benton? I'm sure ye no' here for the good of your health now, are you?"

Saul patted the man on the back. "Relax, John. I'm here to make their lives better, if I can. Have a look at the facilities. See what needs upgrading."

A grunt escaped the Scotsman. "I'll believe that when I see it. There's been no investment here for years. We're run on a shoestring. Health and safety's a big issue. Whatever you're here for, ye'll get nothing past me that's going to jeopardise the health of my men."

"John, John. Not so sceptical, please. I've already told you I'm here to improve things in any way I can. Trust me, won't you?" Saul tried to squeeze a tear-duct so his eyes glistened with sincerity. It just looked like he had a twitch.

"I'm gonnae be blunt with you, Mr Benton.."

"…It's Saul, please."

"Mr Benton will do just fine. I'm gonnae be straight. I don't trust you. Naebody from Head Office has taken any interest in us for years. Why now?"

Saul thought for a moment. "What if I told you – off the record, of course - we were considering investing in a new plant? Sell off the land here. Use the capital to build a state-of-the-art plant further down London Road? You'd have no H&S worries for your men."

He could see the cogs turn in the Union man's brain. He continued. "I reckon it would take no more than two years to construct. You'd be up and running in no time."

The cogs went into overdrive. "I'd say I'd listen to your proposal, Mr Benton. Put it to the men."

"Not yet, please. You're the first to know about this. Local management on site aren't even aware of the plans. I wanted you to be first to know so, please, let me speak to the managers here before you go to your people. It's only courtesy. I'm back here next week. Sit on the idea for a couple of days, please. We don't want to jeopardise anything by letting the cat out of the bag yet, do we?"

John considered the proposal. "Och, why not? It'll give me time to work out the catch."

"You won't find one," Saul assured him. Inwardly, he was elated. He'd sown the first seeds. Next, he would work on explaining how the current plant needed to close. Temporarily, of course. Once EcoHug received the capital from the sale, construction work would begin on the new site. What's more, the workforce would be paid in full in the meantime. Win/win for everyone.

John needn't know the plant's doors would never open again.

"Mr Benton. Saul. You're beginning to win me over. In principle, of course. Let's see what next week brings first."

Saul checked his watch. "Can you recommend anywhere to stay around here? Got nothing to hurry home for. Might experience what a Friday night in Peterborough has to offer."

"There's a Radisson's in the city centre. That's about as good as it gets roond here."

"Sounds good. Anywhere to get a drink?"

"Aye. I can recommend The Pheasant just doon the road. Real ale, if that's your tipple. I usually call in there after work on a Friday. Just for the one, like" He hesitated. "If you promise not to tell the shop stewards, you could join me."

"Do you know, I think I might." Inwardly, he gave himself high-fives, fist-bumps and man-hugs.

Game, set and match.

**

Fate's a curious thing. Kerri was at a crossroads between the end of the worst working week of her life and a step away from a new direction. Only now did she realise how much she enjoyed working with Saul, despite his faults. And now, it was too late. Now, he'd gone for good.

She'd heard the rumours and knew they were true. He'd left the Department. Permanently. The Saul and Patsy double-act were what kept her going. With no sign of Patsy returning, she was stuck with the office girls. The Stepford Wives, as she'd come to know them.

Until fate intervened.

She cleared her desk and packed up her things. When she stepped into the elevator, someone already occupied it. A dark-haired woman in a sharp business suit and a heady perfume. Melissa Beecham.

"Hi." Melissa's greeting was perfunctory.

Kerri pursed her lips in an aborted attempt at a smile.

"It's Kerri, isn't it? Come on, Kerri, cheer up. It's the end of the week. Tomorrow is another day, as someone once said."

The doors slid shut. Kerri didn't know why she said it, but say it she did. "Miss Beecham, I hear Saul Benton's on the move. Is it true?"

"It is. Not sure how you know, but I've no reason to deny it." The elevator stopped. A couple got in and the journey resumed in silence. Three floors down, the couple alighted.

"I don't suppose you'd consider me as Mr Benton's replacement, would you?"

Melissa arched her eyebrows. She looked straight ahead. "Not really, no." The elevator ground to a halt at the Reception level. "But I tell you what. Mr Benton will need an assistant in his new role. I could put a word in for you. Level transfer, mind. No promotion in it for you."

Kerri tried to conceal her delight. "That would be good. Thank you, Miss Beecham."

The CEO stepped out. Kerri forgot it was her floor, too. The elevator continued downwards. She leapt in the air and clicked her heels like Dick Van Dyke doing the Old Bamboo just as the doors opened to expose Cyrus Dilley and his lap-top computer.

**

A portal in time opened up. That's the only explanation Saul came up with. He was sat in a pub occupied exclusively by men. Around each circular table sat three or four workers huddled over a pack of cards. Money – and lots of it – littered the beer-sticky table tops. Saul didn't think places like this still existed. It was a scene lifted from the fifties.

He'd taken off his jacket and tie yet remained as conspicuous as a pyramid in the Arctic. The same pint of Greene King he'd nursed for over forty minutes stood in front of him while John circled the tables, slapping some men on their backs, shaking hands with others, each greeting accompanied by his ubiquitous scowl.

Saul noticed some of the workers left their poker hands long enough to display their own version of the Peterborough scowl in his direction. This was serving him no purpose. He swallowed down the last of his beer and was about to leave when John finally approached him.

"'Nother?" the Scotsman asked.

"No, thanks. Think I'll be making tracks."

"Stay a wee while. I've some news for you." Without waiting for an answer, John raised two fingers towards the barman then pointed them at the table. By the time John dragged a stool to the table, the barman arrived with two foaming glasses.

"I've been taking some subtle soundings. I'm not convinced the men will buy into your idea, if you're asking me."

Saul groaned. "Tell me more."

A commotion arose across the bar; a brief ruckus over a marked card. John stood. "Hey," he growled above the hub-bub. "Will ye no' stop it? I'm entertaining here."

The noise stopped abruptly. Saul was impressed. The Scotsman clearly topped the food-chain.

"Sorry about that. Where was I? Oh, aye. You see, there's a shortage of skilled labour around these parts. Your scientists and your lab technicians and all the clever snooty ones like yourself – nee disrespect, you understand – they live here. But the men I represent travel in. It's the opposite of London. Here, It's the workers who commute." John hesitated, as if Saul understood.

Saul sat back. "Go on," he encouraged.

"Well, where we are now, it's right next to the station. If you relocate out-of-town, they'll need a second commute. It'll mean a longer day. More time away from the wife and bairns."

Saul scanned the bar. "Really? You mean less time to spend in here?"

John ignored the comment. "Doesn't bother me, of course. Wife's never home. Been away a couple of weeks this time." He gave a furtive glance over his shoulder. Leant in towards Saul. "She's management," he whispered. "NHS. Always away on some inspection or other."

His brogue returned to normal. "More importantly, a lot of men will be out of pocket and they won't buy that. I cannae support it, either."

"A pay rise is out of the question, John. Company won't go for that."

"Thing is, Mr Benton. It seems it's not a pay rise many of them want. It's a redundancy package."

Saul's heart skipped a beat. He'd just been presented with an open goal. It wasn't an opportunity he'd spurn, though he tried to downplay it.

"Interesting. I wasn't expecting that. It puts a whole new complexion on things. I'll go away and reconsider what we can do. I'll probably cancel next week's visit and work on things from HQ, but I'll be in touch." He reached into his back pocket. "Here's my card."

The Union man fumbled in his pockets, too. Came out with a crumbled and torn headed notepad. He ripped a sheet out and passed it to Saul.

"Away ye go," John said.

Saul draped his jacket over his shoulders and had his hand crushed once more. He bid his farewells and stuffed the sheet of paper into his pocket.

He wouldn't need that again.

Colin Youngman

DAY THIRTEEN

In close-up, the visceral detail grabbed him by the balls and drew him in. He segmented the image into squares and zoomed into each separate quadrant until the pixilation ruined the view.

In the lower left quadrant, the tip of a thin hair emerged from the prosthetic wound. Intrigued, yet frustrated he couldn't acquire a clear view, Cyrus clipped an image of the strand and saved it onto a clipboard for examination later.

The clock in the bottom-right corner of the screen read 02:15. Cyrus Dilley leant back and closed his eyes, working the possibilities through in his mind. Within seconds, he was asleep.

Cyrus sat up, alert and surprised. His Asperger's meant he rarely fell asleep at will yet the clock showed 06.50. He rubbed his eyes until they smarted before bringing the monitor out of hibernation. The image was still there.

He reached for the mug by his side, wincing at the sour taste of cold coffee. His work could wait. After all, he knew what he was looking at.

He stepped out of his office. There was no motion-sensor lighting in the basement corridor. It was dark as pitch but Cyrus knew his way around the tunnel-like passageways as if it were his home.

He fumbled in his pockets for loose change as he approached the spectre-like radiance of a vending machine. A coin spilled on the floor. He bent to retrieve it. When he stood, a shadow lay across the light.

His fingers snapped open and closed rapidly.

"What are you doing here?"

**

Patsy inched open the door. Odours of lilac and lavender assaulted his senses. "Are you awake?" he whispered. No answer. He closed the door quietly.

Downstairs, he buttered himself a slice of toast while his coffee percolated. Through the window, he watched as spring exposed herself in microcosm.

A couple of old-timers tended their seedlings and bulbs in the allotment gardens with the care of mother-hens. Unfurling foliage, the scent of mown grass and the return of birds all added to the sense of rebirth. Nothing stirred Patsy's emotions as deeply as the arrival of spring. But not today.

Today, his mood was somber as the grey clouds which fled across the sky, pursued by a stiff breeze which dislodged premature blossom and scattered it across the gardens like rose petals on a coffin.

A shudder ran through Patsy. He scraped the uneaten toast into a bin, loaded a tray with his coffee and a pot of tea for his sister, and trudged upstairs.

Patsy tapped on the door. No response. "I've got your tea," his voice soft. He pushed open the door. He felt the tray slip from his grasp. Tried to catch it as it slid away from him. In slow-motion, he watched the tray tumble towards the floor. It clattered on the laminate in a shower of steaming liquid and fragments of china.

Then everything sped-up.

"Damn. I'm sorry, my dear. I didn't mean to startle you," Patsy said to the bed.

An empty bed that hadn't been slept in.

He doubled over as a sudden pain gripped his abdomen.

**

Melissa, Saul and Cyrus sat in the boardroom, the three of them lost in the large room.

"We need to take stock of where we are." She wandered across to a whiteboard. Drew a figure one in green marker pen. Alongside it, she wrote 'Is Pole Star behind our problems?' She swapped pens and wrote 'Cyrus' next to it in blue.

"Number two. Is streamlining our operations do-able, and will it buy us enough time?" She allocated the task to Saul in red pen.

"Three. Is it an inside job?" In pink, she wrote 'Melissa/All'.

"Finally, and most importantly, are those e-mails genuine and where do they come from? Cyrus, perhaps we can start with the last one first?"

Cyrus looked at the board. "One thing first. Can I have my name in red ink? I don't like blue".

Melissa quelled Saul's 'For fuck's sake' and smudged out Cyrus and Saul's name before changing colour. "Sorry, Cyrus. I should have asked."

Saul shook his head. "Ok, now we've got the pretty colours right, can we start? I didn't get back from Peterborough until late and I'd like to check

Steph's settled in ok at her mothers. So, can we get this over with PDQ?"

"It'll take as long as it takes," Melissa chastised. "Mr Dilley, the floor's yours."

Cyrus walked to the whiteboard looking at it rather than his audience. "I haven't started on the e-mail address yet. Before you ask why, I know Mr Benton here was keen to determine whether we need involve the police. I've been working on the photographs first."

"And?" Saul asked, barely keeping his irritation at Dilley's dramatic pause in check.

"The photograph is real."

Saul let out a noisy breath. "Right. We're calling in the police."

"I wouldn't. Not yet."

Saul became animated. "Are you crazy? We've got evidence a modern-day Jack the Ripper slasher's at large and you want us to withhold evidence? That's a crime, man."

Melissa intervened. "Let's talk this through, Saul."

"No. No way. The time for talking's done. I know you want to protect the company's image but alerting the police to this surely puts us in a good light. We're not sending them on a wild goose chase now we know that thing's real."

Cyrus raised a hand to reveal a sweat-stained underarm. "Mr Benton, you really should brush up on your semantics. I said the photograph was genuine. I didn't say it was real. There's a difference."

"Oh for fuck's sake. What are you talking about?"

Melissa stepped in again. "Saul, please. You must understand Mr Dilley doesn't see the world as we see it. Cyrus, please explain what you mean."

"I presume you watch television, Mr Benton." Saul rolled his eyes but nodded all the same. "Good. If you watch say, CSI, you haven't made it up. You've seen it, so the programme is genuine; real actors saying real lines. But the thing itself isn't real. They're not investigating real crimes. It's fiction."

"So?"

"So, it's the same with our 'victim'. The picture isn't faked. It's not a CGI image. It hasn't been tampered or interfered with. It's not a composite. But what it isn't, necessarily, is an image of a dead body. It's a genuine picture of a prosthetic. Now, do you understand?"

Chastened, Saul admitted he did.

Melissa beamed. "Good work, Cyrus. That means we ARE being set-up. Now, we can look to solve this internally."

Cyrus appeared more uncomfortable than usual. In a faint voice, he added, "Please note that I said it isn't 'necessarily' an image of a dead body.

I'm not a pathologist but, all things considered, I'm confident it isn't."

"Then that's good enough for me, Mr Dilley. Saul?"

Saul nodded.

Cyrus began wrapping up his session. "Of course, the e-mails are real. Someone, somewhere, is targeting us. Or, it seems, Patsy MaGill in particular, for reasons unknown. I hope to learn more tomorrow."

He paused to sip from another cold cup of coffee before pointing towards the top of the board. "I suspect the e-mail trail will lead us to Pole Star, which would answer number one. However, let's not jump to conclusions. And we still need to know how they've infiltrated us."

Cyrus moved away from the board, holding a print-off of the fake corpse. As Saul took his place and prepared his update on the Peterborough developments, the IT guru spoke again.

"I'd like to meet whoever did this. I admire them. It takes a special person to do something like this. Even if it turns out to be genuine AND real."

**

The Rat didn't listen to classical music yet, today, the dramatic tones of Prokofiev's Romeo and Juliet was a perfect fit.

The Rat printed off the images and held them up to the light, inspected them with the eye of a forger. These would take pride of place in its lair. Positioned on the blood-spattered wall above the manacles, they were destined to mark the spot where The Rat had come of age.

Why hadn't it thought of this before? Sweet reminiscences of a naked addict in a shower and a pathetic whore in a grave were dependent on a memory that would surely fade. The images in its grasp provided lasting testimony to The Rat's finesse.

The next kill must be special to top this one. Very special.

The Rat ramped up the volume another couple of notches and resumed its research from the pages of a library book plucked from a stack on the floor. It flipped open the polythene-encased cover.

The jacket read: *'The Journey of the Magi. By Thomas Stearns Eliot'*.

The Rat began to recite.

'A cold coming we had of it
Just the worst time of the year
For a journey, and such a long journey
The ways deep and the weather sharp
The very dead of winter.'

The Rat pictured the interior of a concrete chamber in a building on the Gallows estate. In its mind, The Rat searched the room until its eyes settled on the object it searched for.

There, in a corner beneath fresh graffiti, a chest-freezer readied itself for action.

Alley Rat

DAY FOURTEEN

"...Look, I didn't have to call you, you know. You haven't exactly bothered your arse to find out how I'm doing, have you? I just wanted to check that you were ok, but you can forget it. You're obviously doing just fine." He ripped off his headset flung it onto the table. "Christ," he muttered to himself. "Women. Remind me to find a bloke with tits to marry next time."

"I'm not sure I fit all of those criteria." The voice came from behind him, from the open boardroom door.

Saul ran a hand through his hair. "Sorry, Miss Beecham. I didn't see you there."

"So I gather. Things no better, I presume?"

"Not a lot, no. But, on the bright side, it means being stuck in here on a Sunday is not such a bad thing. Besides," he said, looking Beecham up and down, "You don't look too clever yourself."

Melissa wore no make-up, her long face pale. Puckered ridges fringed her mouth while lines like river deltas spread out from the corners of her eyes. Her hair was unkempt. She had on a pair of skinny jeans and a baggy sweater, deck shoes on her feet. She looked more upmarket housewife than cool, calm Chief Exec.

"Touche." She checked her wristwatch. "No sign of Cyrus yet?"

He shook his head. She nodded. They sat in a long silence which grew ever more uncomfortable. It broke when they both spoke at the same time. They gave a chuckle of embarrassment.

"You first," Saul said. "Age before beauty."

"I was just about to say you did well with Peterborough. It looks more promising than I could have hoped."

Saul gave a quick nod of appreciation. "Does that mean I've got my promotion?"

"Let's not get ahead of yourself, Mr Benton. There's a way to go yet." After a moment, she added, "But I do have your assistant lined up. Just in case, you understand. Don't read anything into it."

He looked into eyes that appeared grey and troubled. "You have?"

"Yes. I bumped into Kerri Duncan on Friday. She's not a happy bunny so I suggested she considered working with you."

Saul harrumphed.

Melissa looked surprised. "I thought you two got along fine. Thought you'd be pleased."

"I don't know. She's ok but I was kind of looking at a clean break. Perhaps trying to manage my own workload, control my own diary. Become an AD who seems just a normal guy. If I ever have been normal. I guess I'm also a bit sick of having women tell me what I should do."

The CEO ignored the remark. "You don't think Cyrus is having trouble signing in without a pass for once, do you?"

"Doubt it. Damian's on duty. Vic the Prick's the one he might have trouble with."

"Who?"

Saul chortled. "Victor Pritchard. A bit of a jobsworth." Saul thought he caught a scent of something when the CEO laughed. "Melissa, have you been drinking?"

She stood and walked away from him. "A gin or two. I'm not sleeping. Not easy times, these. For any of us."

"True. I wish I knew what Cyrus had come up with. He should be here now."

"He's probably working from home."

"What, with all the kit he's got down in his Secret Bunker? Why'd he do that?"

Melissa tossed her hair. "A couple of reasons. For example, he knows our systems have been infiltrated. Probably thinks it's safer at home. I believe he's got more IT equipment in his house than Mission Control Houston."

Saul snickered. He believed it was probably true. "And the second?"

She thought for a moment, a pensive look across her face. "No, nothing. It doesn't matter. Besides, he's probably just plugged into some obscure 70s concept album."

"Now, that I can believe." He chortled again. "You know, you're pretty good at reading men, aren't you?"

"I like to think so."

A thought struck him. "Is that why the board consists solely of men?"

She tilted her head. "You're getting warm."

"Pray tell."

"Do you really want to know why I appoint men to senior positions?"

"Yes, I do."

She pulled up a chair and drew breath.

**

The conniving, stinking rotten cow.

Victor Pritchard rocked back-and-forth in his apartment's lone armchair. He'd gritted his teeth so tightly he'd lost a filling. Now, his hands were stiff and aching due to the tightness of his clenched fists.

All he'd wanted was a bit of company from someone prepared to give it him. How could that be wrong, let alone a crime? His good name, his reputation, his standing in the community; all were in jeopardy.

And his job, too. He was an important man. He helped scientists find cures for cancer. Enabled damaged children to live a fuller life. He even helped ensure bitches kept themselves clean each month. Without him, EcoHug could do none of those things. Now, all that was over with.

All because the conniving, stinking rotten cow trapped him.

It wasn't the arresting officer's fault. He was just doing his job. But her? She'd lied to him. Led him into a trap.

Victor Pritchard needed to clear his head. He picked his coat from the floor and strode out into the spring afternoon.

**

"I remember the time you first came to my attention. The way you handled the presentation in London, with little knowledge of your subject matter and even less preparation, really impressed me, Saul. And do you know why? It impressed me because it reminded me of a situation I found myself in not long before I got the CEO permanently."

Melissa sat slightly hunched, her arms in tight folds across her chest. Her words came out quickly, as if they needed escape before she closed the door on them and they were locked away forever.

"My predecessor, Sir Duncan Whitmore, was on long-term sick. He'd overseen the introduction of a controversial cannabis-based treatment for multiple sclerosis. Parliament was in uproar, the Health Secretary forced to resign. I was only thirty-one but I was ambitious and I was bloody good, so I was one of a group who stepped in to pick up the pieces."

She fell silent. Wished she was in her office with the contents of her bottom drawer. Instead, she looked at the EcoHug logo and felt its embrace.

"When a BBC researcher approached me and suggested they run a sympathetic piece on the company, I put myself forward. I thought some positive publicity would be good for EcoHug's recovery and even better for my career." Melissa laughed humourlessly. "That was mistake number one."

Saul Benton watched, hushed, as his CEO drifted off into another world, a world of pain and hurt and betrayal.

"When I got to the studio, everyone was nicey-nicey. Perfect hospitality in the Green Room. Food and drink aplenty. The researcher who'd spoken to me approached with a member of the crew. They ran through a few ground rules. She told me it was live TV. 'Watch your language', she said. 'Don't interrupt the presenter'. 'Be brief; you've only got three minutes.' 'Try not to um and ah' and then, with no warning, 'you're on now.'"

Melissa dug her long fingernails into the palm of her hand. She looked down to see blood seep to the surface.

"It was a nightmare. I was hustled onto an uncomfortable seat in the full glare of hot studio lights. The presenter, an aged woman with oversized glasses and a rapier tongue, ripped into me from the off. 'Miss Beecham, your company's named EcoHug. You bill yourself as the family-friendly pharmaceutical company. How do you reconcile the image you portray with the reality? The reality is, you're not a drug company, are you? You're drug peddlers'. I had barely begun to speak when she said, 'You're avoiding the question, Miss Beecham. Your customers deserve an answer. Your country deserves an answer.'"

Melissa was shaking, now. She began gnawing at the dagger of a fingernail.

"I started to explain that she was referring to one drug out of many, and even Cannadril had helped ease suffering, but she wouldn't let me speak. 'Miss Beecham, are you really trying to defend your company's use of illegal drugs? What example does that set our children?' I tried to use her mention of children as an opportunity to move onto our track-record of reducing childhood obesity but the bitch cut me off. 'I'm sorry, we've run out of time. That was Melissa Beecham, representing the Chief Executive of EcoHug.'"

Saul saw her pain. He reached for her hand. Melisa withdrew it abruptly.

"After the show, I saw the old hag talking to the producers. I marched across to her and barged into her conversation. I really let rip. Didn't hold back. Mistake number two. She fired back with the full 'don't you know who I am?' treatment. Worse, she also wrote a syndicated newspaper column. Three days later, the bitch filled it with garbage about me. Even then, she wouldn't let it lie. I appeared in her column again the next week. Called me a female Pablo Escobar."

Saul spoke for the first time in a long while; a simple, "So, what happened next?"

Melissa Beecham made a guttural sound. "Drink happened, that's what happened. Drink and a breakdown. I was a lush and a jellyfish at little more than thirty. Believe me, Saul, it was a long, long road back from there."

The CEO sniffed away tears that never quite fell. She straightened her back. Sat upright. "But, back I came. Back and fighting. And back with a certainty that women aren't trustworthy. Women aren't even nice. In fact, if the world could continue without them, I'd willingly lead a cull."

**

The prospect of assisting Saul excited Kerri. She'd given it a lot of thought and believed it to be a great career move for her, too. A raised profile, an addition to her CV, working with someone she genuinely liked – most of the time – in the knowledge he'd support her decisions…bring it on.

Only one thing troubled her: the guilt at leaving Patsy without his two closest confidantes. He'd be in the position she'd found herself in last week, and it was a lonely place. Kerri owed Patsy something. The least she could do was break the news to him.

Besides, she wanted to see him. Kerri needed assurances that he was ok; that the cancer wasn't back. A whole week without contact from him was unprecedented. She glanced at her wristwatch. 'A bit early,' she concluded. 'Later. I'll pop over later.'

**

It was Saul who made the decision. "Look, Melissa, for whatever reason, Cyrus isn't going to make it today. Why don't we call it a day? We can't do a great deal without his input."

Melissa blinked. "Huh?" She was still in a different place. She snapped back to the present. "Let me call him first. I don't want any delays on this. If he doesn't pick up, I agree. We'll reconvene in the morning. First thing, mind. No late starts."

She speed-dialled Cyrus Dilley's private number. It rang, and it rang, and rang. She shook her head.

"Lost out to Wishbone Ash?" Saul asked.

"Looks like it. Ok, I'm tired. You're right. Let's call it quits. We'll reconvene tomorrow. All of us." She disconnected the call.

Three miles away, a hand stopped twitching and picked up a call. "Hello? Are you there?"

**

The cloudless sky wore a matt silver finish as late afternoon sauntered into evening and on towards early night.

With the approach of darkness, The Rat's hunger returned. Anticipation of nightfall heightened The Rat's expectations and it loitered impatiently at the chosen location. The script was written; the theatre prepared.

Only the casting remained.

Footsteps approached. The click-clack of heels. A woman. The Rat retreated out of sight. The woman was alone. She paused, her back to the killer, barely ten paces away. What is it they say? 'You're never more than ten steps from a rat'.

But it was still too light. Another thirty minutes, and it would have been perfect. Then the woman was gone, down the hill and out of striking distance. For the first time, The Rat felt frustration.

The next one would pay double.

**

Night had fallen by the time Kerri Duncan reached Patsy's home. The terraced house was in darkness, too, heavy patterned curtains drawn; no sign of life behind them. 'A wasted journey,' she thought. Another thought struck her. What if Patsy really was ill? What if he was lying unconscious on a floor somewhere inside?

Decision reached, she made her way to the rear of the house.

Via an alley alongside his orange front door.

Kerri's movements hadn't gone unnoticed. A pair of eyes watched while the mouth beneath them cursed. The council had been busy. Busy repairing streetlights. The alley was bathed in an orange glow.

Even from its vantage point, The Rat could make out ornamental topiary in pots and the metallic shutters of a garage door. The Rat also saw the girl pause to light a cigarette. Smoke filtered upwards like ectoplasm from her soul.

The alley was far too conspicuous. Yet, at the far end, a black maw waited to swallow prey whole.

When the girl set off towards it, The Rat gave the darkness time to digest her before slinking into the void in pursuit.

DAY FIFTEEN

Two faces peered out of a tenth-floor window. The faces appeared older than the age of their owners. They surveyed the parking lot, watching as it filled. The car they sought wasn't there.

Melissa wrung her hands. "Where the hell is he?"

Saul shrugged. "No point waiting. We need some decisions, Melissa. Let's do this ourselves."

"Five minutes. Give him five more minutes." She moved from the window. Paced the floor while Benton kept watch.

"Hey. Patsy's here, Melissa. There's his car. He's back." The first good news Saul had received all weekend. "We should bring him up to speed."

Melissa nodded. "May as well while we wait for Dilley."

She buzzed Zoe with the request. A moment later, the intercom crackled again.

"He won't be long. He's got a conference call to wind-up."

They waited in silence, each lost in their thoughts, until Zoe poked her head around the door. "Mr MaGill's here for you, Miss Beecham."

Saul and Melissa gasped when they saw him. Grey-faced, red-rimmed eyes, unshaven jowls. His crumpled shirt clashed garishly with the tie. His shoes were unpolished and his socks odd.

Saul looked him over. "Christ, Patsy. What's the matter? You look like shit."

Patsy gave him a wan smile. "Been an awful weekend, guys. Sorry about the appearance. I need to be at work, though."

"Are you sure?" Melissa this time, equally concerned. "You don't look good."

"I'm ok, honest. I lost my sister at the weekend."

Saul and Melissa's faces sagged in pity. "Patsy, I'm so sorry." The CEO rushed to him. Wrapped her arms around him.

Patsy stood stock-still, arms by his side. Realisation dawned. "No, no. Not like that." He almost laughed. "I lost her. I mean, she went missing. I've found her again but I was up most the night searching for her." He saw the look on their faces. "Sorry."

Melissa and Saul let out a lungful of carbon dioxide. "Ya great feckin' eejit, as they say in the land of your forefathers," Saul grinned. "I thought…"

The door burst open. A breathless Cyrus Dilley rushed in lugging a heavy stainless-steel case. "Apologies. You need to see this."

Without further explanation, he opened the case. Two laptop computers emerged followed by a tablet. He set up connections, twiddled with leads, and inserted dongles and memory cards and paraphernalia from a Dr Who convention into various orifices, while the others exchanged puzzled glances.

"You need to see this," he repeated.

A screen burst to life. The company gathered around it. They looked at a screen fringed with pinkish-red; a broad strand ran through the centre, the image blurred, distorted and unrecognisable.

"Is that it?" Saul asked. "I expected the Dead Sea Scrolls, at least."

"Cyrus," Melissa said. "I'm being patient with you, I really am, but how is this relevant to Pole Star and Patsy's e-mails?"

Cyrus looked at them as if they were mad. "I devised a comparison tool. When I ran the image through the software, the program identified the object. What we're looking at here is a mechanoreceptor."

He fiddled with a sonic-screwdriver device. Another screen lit up. "This is how it would look viewed through an electron microscope."

The second screen displayed a bulbous object, its surface pitted with thorn-like spines. He stood back, a satisfied smile on his face, brimming with pride.

Melissa battled with her tolerance levels. "So?"

"You mean you don't know? You haven't realised?" Cyrus shook his head in incredulity. "What we're looking at is a multifunctional sensory appendage."

"Cyrus, really. We don't have time for this."

"We do, Miss Beecham. We do. This," he pointed at the image, "Is the antenna from a cockroach. And the appendage is coated in a viscosity of a type that can only come from one source."

He paused.

"It came from here." He depressed and held the Ctrl button at the same time as pressing a function key. The image zoomed out frame-by-frame.

Once again, it showed the blurred object across a pinkish-red background.

The hair-like strand faded from view as the coloured zone revealed itself to be a jagged-edged hole.

As the image zoomed out, they saw it wasn't a hole. It was a wound.

Further out still, the image showed purple, suppurated skin around the edge of the maw.

Then, a grey-white mass of flesh filled the screen, the wound a chasm within.

Finally, in glorious high-definition Technicolor, the ruined corpse of Suki Chan revealed itself.

"Miss Beecham," Cyrus Dilley announced, "I have to tell you the picture is genuine."

**

All four sat around Melissa's desk in silence. Saul and Patsy sipped water, pale as ghosts. Melissa drank gin. Her eyes glistened with tears.

Dilley didn't understand their reactions. He was fixated by the image. He uttered a word he'd used previously. "Fascinating."

The spell broke. Saul leapt from his chair, eyes wide. He stabbed Dilley in the chest with a finger. "That fucking word again. It's not 'fascinating'. It's horrific. It's madness. Insane. Don't you realise? This is someone's daughter. For God's sake, it could've been Patsy's sister. It could be Melissa."

His breath came in nasal snorts. Saul lowered his voice, a faraway look in his eyes. In a whisper, he added, "It could be Steph."

Then, his anger returned. "And you told us it wasn't real, or genuine, or whatever flowery words you used to explain yourself. But. You. Were. Wrong. You were wrong all along, weren't you? It's not a tailor's dummy. It's a real, live, girl."

The macho Saul Benton cried the tears of a child. "And we've sat on this for days. Never mind the 'golden hour,' the police have lost days. And, all the while, this poor girl was being eaten from the inside out."

Saul slumped into his seat, exhausted. But not for long. All it needed was Cyrus to say, "I don't see what the fuss is about. She was already dead anyway."

Patsy was on his feet before Saul, pinning Benton to his chair. "Saul; it won't help. It really won't. It's just the way he is. Remember our conversation in The Bull? Cyrus is different to most of us, but it doesn't make him heartless and it certainly doesn't make him evil. It does mean he can't empathise, though. That's all. So, cool it, Saul, please. Cool it, yeah?"

Slowly, Saul resisted his instincts. He stilled. Patsy held him for a few moments more, just to be sure.

Melissa spoke. "Gentlemen, we have awkward questions to answer. EcoHug's roasted. Finished. We can't escape this. I should have listened to Mr Benton all along".

She was back under the lights of a TV studio, confronted by an aged presenter in her oversized spectacles. "We must call this in and have the cahoonas to deal with the fall-out."

All eyes turned to Dilley when he said, "I dare suggest that's the last thing we should do. I haven't finished yet."

**

Yesterday's events ran through The Rat's head.

The Rat remembered how it had dumped its victim between a greenhouse and a potting shed. How it looked down upon her with contempt. How, in close-up, it had noticed this one was different.

She was better dressed than the others, not tarty, not too young. But, she'd been in a dark alley by herself at night. That, alone, was sufficient reason to die.

No, that wasn't the problem.

The Rat had slapped the girl across the face. Hard. It reversed the sweep of its hand. And again. The Rat grabbed the girl by the throat and shook. It kicked her prone form.

She didn't rouse.

She didn't rouse because she was already dead.

"No. You can't be," it had hissed. "I'm not ready." It grabbed the girl and shook her again. It made no difference. The girl's head flopped to one side. She really was dead.

The Rat remembered how it brought its hands to its own head. It had spoken to the dead girl. "I had such a good end for you," it whispered. "And you've ruined it. Ruined it. Were you allergic to the ether? Why did you have to die? Why?"

The Rat recalled how, when it discovered the girl had spoiled its fun, the killer's thoughts had drifted to the deep freeze waiting empty in The Gallows. How it had planned to cut off her fingers one by one. Put her in the chiller between amputations. See if it stopped blood flow.

It intended to continue, moving onto her toes, and keep going some more. Keep going, increasing the vitality of the amputations, until she either bled or froze to death.

Or until there was nothing left to amputate.

Now, all the plans were ruined. She'd died too easily.

The Rat remembered the recital it whispered over the body.

"This is how the world ends
Not with a bang but with a whimper."

**

Melissa's voice brought the room back together. Behind screwed-up eyelids, she asked Cyrus what else he had for them. When he locked eyes with each of them in turn, and didn't look away, they knew whatever was coming was seriously bad.

"I've been working on this all weekend. I'm exhausted."

"I sense a 'but'." Saul barely hid his exasperation.

They struggled to hear Dilley's voice. He spoke in a whisper. "I've been working on the e-mails Mr MaGill's received. I've identified the source."

All three spoke at once. "And?"

"It's more difficult than you think. To retrieve an e-mail, a client connects to their respective protocol services by way of an SMTP. A message is sent in the same manner. When a new message arrives in a MAILBOX, the Router determines where and how to send the message…"

Melissa stood. "Cyrus. Cut the crap. Do you know where those e-mails came from?"

"I do."

"For fuck's sake, man. Where? Are they from Pole Star?"

"The sender tried to disguise their location by routing via several exchange servers across the world but, yes, I know where they came from. Close enough."

They looked at him expectantly. He didn't disappoint.

"They came from someone in EcoHug."

They all started talking at once; gabbled, frantic conversations.

"Silence!" Melissa's voice. Firm and assertive. "So, it is an inside job. WHO in EcoHug?"

Cyrus deflated. "I don't know. It could be here, in this office. Or it could be from any of our plants. Birmingham, Peterborough, Cumbernauld; the sender could be anywhere. All I know is it definitely originated via our Home server."

They became deafened by the room's silence, each reeling in the revelation. Once again, Melissa Beecham broke the hush. "Let's take stock. See what we know."

She walked to the whiteboard. Wiped off yesterday's contents. They seemed inconsequential now.

"Ok. We know the photos are both real and genuine, so we have a murder on our hands." She thought of the stock image attached to the first e-mail. "Who knows, there may be more." She scrawled on the board in coded form.

"Two. We know the e-mails came from EcoHug. Which means the killer is one of our own." Melissa shuddered, the realisation only just hitting home base.

"Also, we know for a fact Pole Star is out to ruin us. Are they funding someone in EcoHug?" She wrote 'industrial espionage' / 'insider dealings' followed by a question mark.

"Until we know for sure, none of this gets out. If we can hang it on Pole Star, we do so. We go to police, media, everywhere we can, and we go with both barrels. Until Cyrus provides us with surety, we sit on this. Understand?"

She'd left them in no doubt that they did understand.

"Next, we know Patsy's sister is safe and well..."

"...she's not well, but she is safe," Patsy interjected.

Melissa nodded. "So, why target Patsy? Why come through him if he's not connected to that poor girl?"

Once more, they sat in a befuddled silence, staring at the board; hoping the answer sprung out at them.

Saul swallowed. Phlegm caught in his throat. He coughed. Felt in his pocket for a tissue. Touched something else. A piece of notepaper. A thought struck him like an uppercut.

"My God."

"Saul? You onto something?"

He stared into space for a while. "I've got a call to make."

He dialled from where he sat. The conversation was brief. He asked only two questions. Saul disconnected. Three pairs of eyes studied him.

"Well?"

He spoke in measured tones. "There's a guy I met in Peterborough. His wife works away a lot. He rarely hears from her when she's away. She was due back yesterday. As you may have gathered from the conversation, she didn't turn up. He's not worried. I am."

The room fell icy cold.

"There's more, isn't there?"

"Yes, there is. As you heard from the call, his name's John. I also know his surname. What I didn't know, until now, is whether he had a middle name."

Saul stared out the window; out towards the car park, but he saw only the mutilated remains of a girl.

"His name's John McGill. With a 'c', not an 'a'; but McGill nonetheless. John Patrick McGill"

His gaze returned to three slack-jawed faces.

"What if they've got the wrong Patsy MaGill?"

DAY SIXTEEN

The bedding resembled a rope ladder. Saul unknotted himself from it and scratched his head. 'God, what a night.'

He'd barely slept. Thoughts raced through his brain like hounds after a fox. Saul pictured the remains of the poor girl and reeled in the knowledge that the person responsible probably worked for his company. His thoughts turned to Steph, and the fear he'd experienced when his imagination let him believe it could have been her with the open chest. Or belly. With little Roland inside.

Saul propped himself up and guzzled from a tumbler of tepid water. Something else troubled him. Something which lay like an object submerged beneath shifting waters. Something visible but unrecognisable.

When Saul's thoughts drifted to John McGill and his missing wife, he forced himself into the shower, determined to scrub them away.

At least John McGill had slept, but at this moment it didn't feel like it. He awoke with cramps in both legs, a spasm in his back and a stiff neck. He lay on a sofa alongside a stinking tray of half-eaten kebab meat and an empty bottle of Whyte & MacKay.

He squinted at his wristwatch. 'It's well seen she's no' back yet,' he groaned. He buried his face in the seat's arm and vowed he'd have one more hour.

His near-namesake, Patsy MaGill, rose early. Puzzled, horrified and not a little angry that he should be associated with the abomination he'd witnessed yesterday, he saw no point staying in bed. He couldn't sleep.

Besides, things needed his attention.

He opened the window, took a gulp of fresh air, and looked out over the small garden and the expanse of allotments beyond. It was a scene he treasured, both for the view and the serenity the location provided his sister.

"You know', he said to himself. "I'd kill to protect this."

In a darkened room, Cyrus Dilley had no idea whether it was night or day. He'd been sitting at his horseshoe workstation for hours. In front of him, two monitors displayed the same gory image, albeit from different angles, in pornographic detail.

Dilley's attention wavered between the monitors and a third displaying line upon line of complex code. His fingers pummelled a keyboard. More lines appeared; an intricate blend of symbols, numbers and abbreviations.

Dilley paused for a split second, index-finger poised above the ENTER key. He hit it. The screen scrolled down, page after page of flashing icons and nonsense text.

The screen cleared. He was in. The profile of every employee of EcoHug was at his fingertips. He had access to their e-mail folders. Remote access.

He could do anything he wanted.

He just couldn't make another mistake.

**

Another familiar face had been up all night. Victor Pritchard. His shift work meant he was in a permanent state of jet-lag, but that wasn't what kept him awake. Not this time. It was the fear of a stained reputation. He was sure news of his arrest hadn't leaked out but, when it did, he was sure he'd never work for EcoHug again.

Vic the Prick had wandered the streets all night, his mind in turmoil. He'd taken in every quadrant of the city while he tried to quell his fears. Night had barely fallen when he passed the regency quarter, while by the time he reached the city centre, the pubs and clubs were starting to shoo out revellers along with the empties.

The area around the cathedral was as quiet as its graveyard, and the hulking mass of Mother's Mound snuffed out the silver glow of a crescent moon as Pritchard made his way along the canal's arrow-straight towpath.

Dawn approached with the stealth of a cat burglar as he rested a while on a stone bench. It was only when his thoughts drifted to the wretched policewoman who'd lied to him that he ventured onwards. Victor smiled to himself when he thought of ways he'd like to pay her back.

From behind a coppice, as if in a sign from the Gods, he spotted the rotating red and blue lights of emergency vehicles. They appeared stationary.

He heard voices up ahead, the sounds of activity. A figure appeared not twenty paces ahead, walking away from him. The figure passed beneath a dim light, half-turning to answer a command from the right. Pritchard gasped. He'd seen the profile before. Sitting alongside him in the passenger seat of a car on The Gallows estate.

He ducked to his right, away from the canal, behind the concrete struts of a footbridge. He hunkered down, watching the scheming bitch of a policewoman's movements.

His hand rested on a pile of rubble, concrete crumbled from the bridge support. He wrapped his fist around it. Weighed it in his hand. And prepared himself.

So focused was he on seeking revenge on the WPC, he was oblivious to her two colleagues approaching from behind.

**

The Cor Anglais solo from Dvorak's Ninth Symphony roused Melissa Beecham from a fitful sleep. A long-fingernailed hand emerged from beneath the bedding and fumbled for the alarm switch. Classic FM fell silent. She wished she could have done the same to the shits outside her apartment last night.

Ever since the canal-side had fallen foul of the nation's fetish for waterside developments, and three bars and a gaggle of cafés and restaurants had opened half a mile upstream, Melissa's sleep patterns were at the whim of their clients.

Last night had been particularly rowdy. From two a.m., she'd been kept awake by raised voices, car doors slamming, and goodness knows what else. Sleep had taken her only an hour before Dvorak came calling.

She sat on the edge of her bed for a moment, shook out her hair, and stepped naked to her refrigerator. She poured herself fresh orange juice and listened to the song of blackbirds until wakefulness settled.

Still naked, Melissa padded to the curtains, reached up and drew them open. Only to whip them closed again when she was met by the sight of two frogmen staring in at her.

**

The three men checked their watches. "She's late," said one.

"Should we start without her?" asked another.

The third played with his fingers.

They all checked their watches for a second time.

The door burst open. Melissa Beecham strode in, pink cheeks, uncombed hair, little make-up. "Sorry I'm late. I couldn't get the motorbike out until the police removed their tape."

"Come again?"

"Some drunken idiot tried to swim the canal last night, I guess. Don't think he made judging by the police presence. Right," she clapped her hands, "Let's get down to business. Plan of action for today, guys." The men raised clipboards and drew out notepads. "I'm handing over the running of EcoHug until we get to the bottom of this. I'll be speaking to Nicholas Irvine to tell him the ship's his. Wrap it up under the pretext of a thank you for his service before he retires."

She thought for a moment. "It's the least I can do because I suspect he'll find his pension pot's smaller than expected once we release the latest trading figures. Saul, I want you to investigate John McGill. See if you can find out what's going on with him and his wife."

"Do you want me down in Peterborough?"

"No, not likely. Too much to sort here for you to go AWOL. Do it by telephone, at least until we know if there's anything in your theory."

Saul nodded. Made a few notes.

"Cyrus, I want you down in the IT hub. Get a message to Lynnette Szydlowski. Find some excuse for her to check the e-mail servers while you focus on the Pole Star bug. They've upped the ante so no point hanging back now."

Cyrus opened his mouth to speak but the CEO had already moved onto Patsy. "As for you, Patsy, until Saul's checked out the John McGill thing, I'd like you to think of anyone who may have a grudge against you. Schooldays, private life, family, friends, work colleagues; the works. As many as you can think of."

Beecham checked her watch again. It read 9.40. "We'll meet back here in one hour for a progress check. Come on, move it." She shooed them out of her office as if they were flies at a horse's arse.

**

Patsy MaGill stared at a blank sheet of paper for the first half of the hour. He was clueless. He'd been popular at school in a quiet, unobtrusive sort of way. Never bullied, never fought, no disciplinary issues. Nothing.

He'd had one or two girlfriends over the years. More than one or two, if truth be known, but they hadn't lasted long. They all came into his life as friends, initially, and they left as friends, too. No acrimonious break-ups, none of his ex-partners were in a relationship when he met them, so no jealous exes.

As for family, his parents were both only children. No aunts or uncles, no cousins in the picture. There was his sister, but he lived with and cared for her. He'd know.

Friends? Several good acquaintances but no really close friends, and certainly none who'd crossed the other side and become an enemy.

Which left colleagues. Patsy always got on well with those he worked with. He'd helped boost many a career, he was affable and approachable. At his annual assessments, the phrase most often used to describe him were 'a loyal team player.'

Yet, someone somewhere in his life felt compelled to make him the target of vile messages. Possibly involving murder.

Saul had to be right. It must be mistaken identity. It must be John Patrick McGill.

But Melissa would be expecting him to start somewhere. He recalled a recent conversation with Kerri Duncan. 'He's changed', she'd said.

With a heavy heart, on a sheet of paper on his clipboard he wrote the name 'Saul Benton.'

The IT man sat at his horseshoe workstation. His fingers flew over the keyboard, typing in various codenames and numerical sequences. The legend 'we're working on it' appeared on-screen. Only then did he sit back while the kit did its work.

No way was he bringing Lynnete into this. This was his baby. She couldn't be trusted with a task so important. She could stick to running the helpdesk, dealing with staff, placating angry clients. The kind of work more suited to a woman.

While he waited, he studied a second screen; a screen containing the image of a woman. Or, more accurately, what had once been a woman.

The black screen burst into life. He was in. Not into the Pole Star database, but EcoHug's own e-mail server.

Saul disconnected the call without leaving a voicemail. After all, how do you casually say 'Hi. I think your wife's had her tits ripped off; call me when you get this?'

He rubbed the centre of his forehead until it turned red. The sheer madness he'd become embroiled in threatened to engulf him. Before it did, his phone rang. The display showed 'caller unknown.' He took it anyway.

The voice at the other end queried his pick-up with a "Hello?"

"Hello," he said back.

"Who is this?" A woman's voice.

"Excuse me, but you called me. Shouldn't I be the one asking the question?"

"Don't play silly buggers with me." The profanity was at odds with the quiet, cultured voice.

"I think you must have the wrong number."

"I don't think so. You're the one who dialled first."

Saul hesitated. A lightbulb moment. His heart-rate increased. "Is that Mrs McGill?" he asked, as much in hope as expectation.

"It is. You've just rang my husband's phone. Are you the one responsible for the state he's in? I come back to a house like a pig-sty and a comatose slob of a husband. Hello? Hello. Are you there?"

She was talking to herself. Saul Benton was already racing around the room punching air.

**

"Right. What we got? Saul, you first, please."

"It's not John McGill's wife."

"Thank the Lord. Are you sure?"

"Yes. I've just spoken to her. She's home and she's fine. Well, she's pretty bloody pissed off with John, but other than that, she's A OK."

The occupants of the room nodded in relief. Until it dawned on Patsy the revelation meant he was the target. He blanched. The others realised it, too, and looked towards him.

Melissa tried to reassure him. "It's ok, Patsy. You know your sister's safe. It seems the killer is using you as a way of warning us. Why you, we don't know. And at least you haven't been subjected to any more e-mails."

"Actually, that's not quite true."

Three heads swung towards Cyrus Dilley. "This was on the server awaiting delivery." He passed a sheet of paper to Melissa.

Patsy took a seat. "What does it say?"

Melissa read from the script.

"The nymphs are departed
And their friends, the loitering heirs of city directors;
Departed, have left no address
By the waters of Leman I sat down and wept."

"Eliot again?" Patsy asked.

She nodded. "The Wasteland, again. From the Fire Sermon."

"Is that all? I mean, no text? No threats?"

"No, not on here, there isn't. Cyrus, was there a covering message?"

Dilley shook his head, dandruff spilling to the floor. "No. That's all."
She looked off into space, trying to make sense of it. The intercom buzzed. "Not now, Zoe."
"But Miss Beecham…"
"No buts. I'm not to be disturbed."
Seconds later the door opened. Zoe again. "I'm sorry, Miss Beecham. But you're needed. Now."
The CEO rolled her eyes. "One moment, gentlemen."
She stepped outside. A man and a woman approached her. "This had better be good," she warned them.
"Melissa Beecham? I'm Detective Superintendent Devaney and with me is Detective Sergeant Nazar. We'd like to ask you a few questions."

**

For the next twenty minutes, the police officers quizzed Melissa about her movements over the last forty-eight hours, whether she'd heard or seen anything unusual. She told them about the ruckus outside last night, about the frogmen – but, of course, they already knew that – and, finally, about the e-mail.
The officers looked at one another, asked who'd sent and received it. Melissa answered the element she was able.
Finally, Nazar passed Devaney two glossy-backed sheets. "Do you recognise either of these two people?" the senior officer asked, flipping the sheets towards the CEO.
The room span in kaleidoscope colours as Melissa's knees buckled.

**

"…it doesn't make any sense." The three men pored over the e-mail message.
"It does. It couldn't make more sense."
All eyes turned to the door. "Holy Mother of God," Patsy said at the sight of Melissa furniture-walk to her seat and drop herself into it. "What's up?"
Melissa took a slug of gin, followed by another. She screwed her face up and offered it to the others. "Take it. You'll need it," she urged when the men declined.
"The extract makes sense. The commotion down by the canal? They found a body."
The room stilled instantly.

Melissa began to weep. Her shoulders rose and fell in heaving shudders. Saul was first to her. Put an arm around her.

"I guess that's sad," Cyrus said in his detached manner. "But what's that got to do with the poem?"

Melissa's response didn't make any sense. "Departed," she said. "Friends. City directors. *By the waters I sat down and wept*," she quoted, crying so much her tears smudged the paper.

She looked at each in turn. "The body. It was Kerri. Kerri Duncan. Our Kerri."

Patsy swore. Saul grabbed the gin bottle and downed it. Even Cyrus appeared moved.

No-one spoke for a full minute. Then Melissa fixed Patsy with her eyes. "They want to talk to you about it, Patsy."

"Me?" Genuine shock followed by outrage. "They can't think it was me. It wasn't me. Who could think I'd do that to Kerri?"

Melissa tried to smile. "No, sorry, Patsy. I should have picked my words more carefully. They just want to ask you about the e-mail. They know it wasn't you."

Relief. Then, "But how do they know?"

"Because they know who did it."

"And?"

"It's over. They've arrested Victor Pritchard."

DAY SEVENTEEN

Saul Benton was first to arrive. He sat on the long narrow balcony of The Boatman's Lodge watching out over the waters from where Kerri Duncan had been hauled twenty-four hours earlier.

Melissa Beecham had closed the EcoHug HQ for the day out of respect. She, Saul, Patsy and Cyrus discussed what to do. They felt a quiet drink together, sharing memories of Kerri, was only right and proper.
Melissa had proposed a coffee shop out of deference to the tea-total Cyrus but Saul and Patsy said they needed a drink. Melissa was secretly pleased. The location had been subject to debate, whether the canal-side bar was too close to home, too maudlin a spot. Eventually, they decided unanimously nowhere was more appropriate.

He took another slug of his ale and watched flies play chase in the spring sunshine.

A chair screeched alongside him. "You holding up, Saul?"

He looked into eyes full of concern, eyes hooded with tiredness, eyes set wide apart in a long face.

"Not really, if I'm honest." He finished his beer with a sigh.

Melissa slid another in front of him. Ice tinkled in her own glass as she set it down. She looked over the ribbon of water before them. "Looks so innocuous, doesn't it?"

He nodded. "Why Kerri, Melissa? What had she ever done to Pritchard?"

"I doubt we'll ever know, unless he decides to talk."

Saul chewed his bottom lip. "I really liked her, Melissa. I feel dreadful for not being ecstatic when you told me about her being my assistant. I feel so guilty."

"Don't be, Saul."

"I guess. But the last couple of weeks, we'd had words. I wish I'd just shut my mouth. Wish I hadn't upset her so. How many people go to their grave ignorant of what others really think of them?"

Melissa held the silence for a full minute. "A few days ago, you asked me something. About London."

He turned to face her. Held his breath. "I did."

"No. We didn't."

He let the breath out in a long, slow whistle. Closed his eyes. Tilted his head back. "Thank you, Melissa. I needed to know. Steph and me, we may be finished, but I've tortured myself over whether we, you know? I've messed other women around, but not her. I've tried so hard to remember. I really have." His eyes moistened.

"You miss her, don't you?"

He didn't reply. Just stared into the murky waters of the canal.

"Call her, Saul. Tell her how you feel." She followed his gaze towards the canal. "Tell her before it's too late."

**

Patsy and Cyrus arrived together. They pulled up seats, Cyrus to Melissa's left, Patsy to Saul's right. All faced the canal.

"On the hard stuff already?" Saul asked with a nod to the amber liquid in Patsy's tumbler.

"Just the one to start with." He raised his glass and saw the sun tweak its contents, the burnt amber Connemara's turning to rich gold and back again. He smacked his lips as the complex flavours burnt his tongue.

Cyrus sipped lemonade from a tall glass. He looked less tired than of late, though the grey in his hair outnumbered the black today.

Long, awkward silences punctuated their conversation until Melissa slid shut the glass doors separating the veranda from the handful of early-lunchtime diners inside.

She set the scene for the day as if she were presenting a workshop. "We're here to remember Kerri, and to appreciate the times we spent with her, but I think we need to clear the air before that's possible."

Saul and Patsy nodded their agreement. Cyrus played with his fingers.

Melissa stated the obvious. "We've lost Kerri and there's no bringing her back. It's also fair to say we're all partly responsible in some way." She raised a hand to suppress dissent. "I'm sorry, gentlemen, but we are. Me more than any of us. I could've stopped this if I'd gone to the police straight away but I was more concerned with the business. That's something I have to live with for the rest of my life."

The men didn't disagree. She continued. "But, we're culpable of even more. We know Kerri isn't the first. We've covered up an obscenity." She pictured the corpse of Suki Chan, and then remembered something DS Devaney told her. "Quite probably, there's been more than one. The question is, do we want to reveal everything we know?"

Patsy was first to speak. "I think we should."

Saul disagreed. "What good would it do? It won't bring Kerri or anyone else back. All we'd do is hammer the final nail in EcoHug's coffin." He winced at the inappropriate phrase. "More importantly, we'd all…" in the nick of time, he avoided saying 'dig our own graves', "Find ourselves under arrest."

"To be honest, Saul, I don't care. It's the right thing to do."

Saul fixed Patsy with a stare. "That's as may be but, even if you don't worry what will happen to your sister, I've got a baby to think of, and I do care how it'll affect him. What sort of start in life would he have with his Dad under arrest? Probably in prison, even." A shudder crawled over him. "No, I say we keep quiet. They've got him now. There'll be no more killings and, as Melissa said, nothing will bring Kerri back."

Patsy saw his point. "Cyrus, what about you? You're probably incriminated in this more than anyone. Your digital fingerprint's all over the systems."

Cyrus took a sip from his lemonade. Rolled an ice-cube around his mouth. Let it slide back into the glass. "They won't find any trace of me. I'm far cleverer than them."

Saul steepled his fingers. Patsy battled his conscience. Melissa made the decision.

"We keep quiet."

**

The afternoon drew on and, as always happens with wakes, the atmosphere lightened. They laughed, joked, spoke warmly of Kerri, picked on her faults in a good-natured way, and they drank.

The quartet ordered food to soak the drink, but only Cyrus had the appetite to finish his meal. In the heat of the afternoon, time drifted by as lazily as the waters of the canal below.

Intermittently, when they were the only ones on the balcony, the conversation returned to Kerri and Vic the Prick; the emotion less raw.

"I always thought he was a tosser but, really, what makes a person do something like that, out-of-the-blue?" Patsy's question was rhetorical but Melissa chose to answer. Answer with a question.

"What makes you think it was out the blue?"

The men turned their heads in her direction. Their look demanded an explanation.

"That DS guy, Delaney or Devaney, or whatever," she paused to sip from a refreshed glass of gin. "He asked me if I knew Pritchard had been arrested a couple of days ago for kerb-crawling. Also, another girl from the same pitch on The Gallows estate hasn't been seen for over a week."

Saul let out a low whistle. He'd joined the dots. "You mean, you think the girl in Patsy's e-mail?" he drifted off without finishing his question.

Melissa set down her glass. "It's quite possible."

They let her words sink in. But Melissa hadn't finished. "There's more. They found Pritchard at the spot where they recovered Kerri's body. He was about to attack a WPC."

Patsy walked to the balcony railings. "I can't get my head around this. He was working security, Goddamnit. For EcoHug. All the time, he was right under our noses."

Another thought hit Patsy like a truck. "What about the first e-mail? Jesus, the first e-mail I got. There'll be another one."

Melissa nodded. "Yep. There is," adding quickly, "Probably."

Silence followed. Cyrus broke it.

"Same again, everyone?"

**

As the sun fell towards the horizon and the bar claimed a new breed of clientele, Melissa beckoned Saul towards her. He leant close, his breath tinged with alcohol, his eyes glassy.

"You need to make a call. Tell Steph how much she means to you. Before you slur too much. Before she thinks it's the drink talking. And before it's too late."

Saul continued to look into Melissa's eyes. "What if she doesn't mean everything to me? What if I wanted to move on?"

Melissa pulled away from him. "I'm already too late, aren't I? That's the drink talking right there. Now, go. Do it. And that's an order, Benton."

He gave a long sigh before strolling to the end of the veranda, Samsung in hand.

When he returned, Cyrus was berating Patsy over his lack of interest in Artificial Intelligence. He needed rescuing.

"Hey, Patsy." Saul said "I hear Finnegan wouldn't let his wife get a Labrador for the kids. He said too many of their owners went blind."

Patsy laughed. "That's the Saul we all know and love."

Melissa gave a girlish giggle, though she saw through Benton's act. "Well?" she asked. "How'd it go?"

His mood changed. "I couldn't get past her mother. Abi said Steph was moving on. I wasn't to upset her. She said I was drunk. That it confirmed everything Steph had said about me." He retook his seat unsteadily. "But I did tell Abi to let Steph know I love her."

Melissa slid her arm through his. "I'm sorry, Saul."

He exhaled through his nose.

"Ok, guys. I think we all need some food." He dished out menus as if they were frisbees. "If we choose from the pizza section, they're on me. And, Patsy – we're all getting them cut into six slices. Last time I ate one with an Irishman, he wanted it cut in four. Said he wasn't hungry enough for six."

All but Cyrus roared with laughter, and Melissa rested her head on Saul's shoulder.

**

They tackled their meal with gusto. As one waitress cleared their table of dirty plates and cutlery, and another collected a snake of empty glasses, Patsy decided he'd call it a night. Cyrus said he would get off, too.

Saul persuaded them to have one for the road. "Good men. This last round's on me. What are we all having?"

A voice joined the conversation from behind. "My, quite a reunion we've got going on here, haven't we?"

They turned to face the interloper.

"Make mine a bitter," Victor Pritchard said.

DAY EIGHTEEN
AM

As an adolescent's mood changes overnight, so did the weather. Drab grey skies welcomed daybreak. Bleak drizzle deposited buds of moisture on car roofs where they lay like tears on a bereaved one's cheeks.

Head down, huddled up and protected from the Scotch mist, a figure walked the silent streets. It could have been anyone. But this was neither any street nor anyone.

The street was on The Gallows estate. And this was The Rat.

Denied the pleasure of its last victim, this one would be just right. There'd be perfection in planning, execution, and choice of quarry. This would be the best yet.

Malevolence grew within. Malevolence and something more. A hunger. A need. The Rat eased open the shutters. They gave with a metallic scream. The killer turned sideways and squeezed through a gap before heaving the shutters back. A quick check to ensure the gap was sealed, and it scurried up to its third-floor lair.

It emptied the contents of its bag onto the bare floor. Searched through them until it found what it wanted. Looked around the chamber. Identified a suitable location.

It shook the canister in its hand. Depressed a button. Soon, the task was complete.

The Rat stood back and admired its handiwork, a blank space in the crumbling wall filled with lurid purple writing.

'The only hope, or else despair
Lies in the choice of pyre or pyre —
To be redeemed from fire by fire.'

Perfect. Just perfect.

**

Saul ran a comb through sodden hair. Melissa Beecham's office was the least attractive place for him this time of day, but here he was. Melissa was with him, also wet, also hung-over.

They drank strong coffee whilst awaiting the others.

"Bit of a turn-up for the books, wasn't it?" Saul's words were laced with heavy understatement. "Pritchard turning up like that, and all."

Melissa didn't reply. She just stared towards the window, watching raindrops squirm like transparent maggots down its surface.

At length, she spoke. "What are we doing, Saul?"

"Nothing. We're doing nothing. It's already done."

She lowered her head in grim resignation. "You think the police may have got it wrong?"

"Not a chance. They wouldn't risk letting Pritchard go if they had any doubts. If he killed again, they'd be shafted. No, I believe what he said. It's not him. He admitted kerb-crawling. He admitted stalking the officer who'd set him up. They've done him for both of those. They must be sure he didn't kill Kerri."

The silence between them lasted forever. Or, at least until Cyrus Dilley joined them. They nodded an unspoken greeting to the T-shirted IT man.

He, alone, accepted Pritchard's release matter-of-factly. "We've still got the same questions to answer. Whether it's an inside job, is there Pole Star involvement, both, or neither. The only fact we do know is that someone in EcoHug knows the truth."

A dishevelled Patsy joined them, popping painkillers into his mouth.

"Thought you'd be feeling rough today," Saul empathised.

"I only wish it was a hangover." Patsy touched his stomach region. "War wound's playing up again."

Saul looked concerned. "You're definitely all right, aren't you?"

Patsy arched his eyebrows. Set his mouth. "Hope so." Before adding, "Yes, of course I am."

Saul shot him a look but Melissa interrupted.

"Gentlemen. Now we're all here, I want to tell you, strictly off the record, I can't do this any more. I know we'll be shot with shit over this. And rightly so. I've been there once and can't put myself through it again. Once this is over, I'm quitting."

All three men voiced their protests at once.

"I appreciate your support; thank you. But I'm not prepared to let myself become ill again." She cast a tell-tale peep towards the bottom-drawer. "I'll see this through, but my mind's made up."

She gave them each a smile. "I'm going away. For a long time."

**

Come lunchtime, Melissa Beecham asked her three confidantes to go their separate ways. "I need to get out of this place for a few hours. I think you should, too. Give ourselves space from each other. Let's give it a couple of hours. See you back here."

She joked she didn't want them planning any elaborate leaving surprises. In reality, she wanted them apart in case they hatched a plan to keep her at the company.

Melissa ensured they'd all left the building before she set off for a long walk to clear her head. She raised her umbrella against heavy rain and headed out with her head filled with memories of her time in EcoHug.

She smiled at the good times, took pride in how she'd overcome periods of adversity, and totted up her many achievements.

Rain bounced off puddles at her feet, cars made whooshing noises as they splashed through standing water, everything sounded quiet, more hushed than in the vibrancy of yesterday's sunshine.

Until she realised the silence was due to where her feet had taken her. She was in an area deserted like the aftermath of a war zone. She was on The Gallows estate. Outside the old EcoHug building.

Saul Benton also stood outside a quiet building. But this was no disused industrial unit. This was a residential area in a leafy suburb. He stood outside the home of Abigail Miller, looking for signs of either her or her daughter, Steph Benton. He found none, but he'd continue searching. He had to find her.

While Saul's thoughts lay with his wife, so Patsy's were on his sister. What if Saul wasn't wrong? What if the tumour had returned? He sat on a bench in Elton Plaza, barely noticing the dampness soak through his trousers. Who would look after her after he was gone? He lowered his head towards his knees, rested the palms of his hands over his face.

And missed Victor Pritchard whistle a happy tune as he sauntered by.

Cyrus Dilley left a coffee shop outside the cathedral, in the shadow of Mother's Mound. Rain dripped off his forehead. The dark-coloured T-shirt clung to him.

Dilley felt in his bones this was the wrong place. He scanned right and left. To the right, he saw a patch of parkland. Often filled with sunbathers in summer, it was lonely and forlorn in the Spring rain. Nothing here.

Dilley switched his attention westwards, towards the shopping district and, beyond and to its left, the industrial area.

The left. Of course!

It was time he started work.

**

The Rat liked the rain. The murk and gloom made finding prey easy. People were less observant. They stared at the floor when they walked, buried their heads in hoods or beneath umbrellas. They missed so much life around them. Life, and death.

The Rat prepared a daytime strike.

It scurried through the mid-day thoroughfares towards its hunting ground. The streets, normally bustling in this part of the city, were lifeless, as if in some strange way the coming of the rain had dried them up.

The Rat turned left off Main Street, avoiding Elton Plaza, then took a shortcut into a slender alleyway. And there, not fifty yards ahead, it spotted her; so fat, so big, she could hardly walk, let alone run.

A filthy, obese pig. Ripe for sticking.

Instantly, The Rat's senses elevated to a higher plane. It noted, without conscious thought, that a sharp bend in the alley obscured the view from the main street. Ahead, the far end of the lane ended in a tiny courtyard, with only a footpath for entry and egress. The surrounding buildings backed onto the courtyard. No windows.

Best of all, a couple of freshly-cleaned wheelie-bins stood in the courtyard. Just the right size to hold and transport a body once The Rat overpowered her.

The killer's gait increased. It noticed the woman wore earplugs. She was tuned in to music, not her safety. Water splashed over The Rat's shoes, soaking feet and ankles

It didn't care. A warm fire waited.

The distance between them closed rapidly. The Rat's breathing became ragged, more nasal. Goosebumps rose on its flesh, pupils dilated, adrenalin coursed.

Barely more than two-arm's length away now. The Rat reached for a blade. No ether this time. It couldn't lose another. The woman sensed something. She hesitated. Half-turned as the blade rose to meet her cheek.

The Rat spun the woman round. It saw she wasn't fat. She was pregnant.

The Rat saw something else. It saw her face contort; first in puzzlement, then in fear. And, finally, recognition.

"You!" Steph Benton gasped.

DAY EIGHTEEN
PM

They were all late back to Melissa's office. Patsy MaGill was first to arrive, fresh from a check on his sister. His eyes contained a tinge of yellow, his face sallow.

"This is taking its toll on you, isn't it?" Melissa asked, concerned.

He coughed. Swallowed thick phlegm. "I'm used to a quiet life. I suppose all this was bound to catch up on me, eventually. This weather doesn't help, either"

She looked at him long and hard. "As long as that's all it is."

Patsy touched his abdomen again. "I'll get it checked out, I promise. But, as far as I know, that's all it is."

Melissa opened her mouth to speak but Saul's entrance interrupted her. "Bloody pissing down out there. Blimey, you ok, Patsy? I've seen healthier-looking folk in a cemetery."

"I've been telling him that. Not quite as bluntly, but the same message."

Patsy rolled his eyes. "Stop fussing, will you? I'll be ok."

Zoe buzzed Cyrus through. He was wettest of all. "Christ, Cyrus," Saul said "You entered a wet T-shirt competition during lunch? Look at the state of you, man."

"I like rain," came the simple explanation.

They stood around in silence. Finally, Melissa spoke. "Listen, I'm staring at a blank page here. Unless anyone's got any ideas what to do next, I propose we go back to other stuff. Saul, why don't you do the sums on the Peterborough closure? It's got to happen regardless. And Cyrus – you resurrect the system interrogation. Look for signs of Pole Star. I don't give a toss now whether they know what we're up to.

"What about me?" asked Patsy.

"You, Mr MaGill, can get yourself checked over. Put your mind at rest. Make that appointment, then get yourself home."

He gave her a meek smile. He appreciated her thoughtfulness.

"As for me, gentlemen, in case you're wondering, I'm going to sit here and drink my gin."

**

Patsy did as he was told. He made an appointment with Dr Oman for tomorrow, drove home and parked up as close to his house as he could. It was still afternoon, yet dark as night, and streetlights blazed in the alley alongside his orange front door.

The front of his house was in darkness, so he headed for the alley. He stood aside to allow an old-timer in cloth cap and baggy denims to pass. The old man touched his cap in deference, exchanged unpleasantries about the weather and its impact on his vegetable patch, and failed in an attempt at lighting a soggy roll-your-own.

Patsy waited until the man exited the alley safely before he moved on. At the lane's head, he veered left. Here, the cobbled lane turned onto a roughly-hewn gravel path from where he could see the garden lit up from the standard lamp in the window.

Except, this time, he couldn't. The garden wasn't lit up. Nor the standard lamp. Nor anything else in the house. It stood dark, empty and forlorn.

Patsy groaned aloud. He knew what it meant.

He'd have to find her again.

**

Back in EcoHug HQ, Melissa Beecham was true to her word. She drank gin. Not copious amounts, but enough to remind her of the bad days. For today, she'd drink just enough.

She spun three 360-degree rotations in her chair, made a 'wheee' noise, and flushed when she saw Saul Benton watching from the door.

"Having fun, are we?"

"The life of a Chief Executive is tough to bear," she smiled. "Play your cards right, and you might find out one day."

"Do you know, I'm not sure I want that anymore. All the politics, the profit-motive, using people as pawns. That's how all this started, isn't it? Pole Star using Patsy?"

"Objection, m'lud. Conjecture."

"Well, ok. I'll give you that one. But take the whole Peterborough thing. It's people's lives we're playing with. And I'm as guilty as anyone. I lied to John MGill. I used him, blatantly. Yes, I got what I wanted. But is it worth it? You know, whenever I think of Kerri, I wonder if she'd still be alive today if we'd just let Pole Star do what they wanted. Was her death a coincidence? Or is the saying right – are they're really none so blind as those who see?"

Melissa raised her glass, swivelled her chair once more. "Bravo, Mr Benton. Admirable use of a proverb. Or is it an idiom?" She shrugged. "Admirable use of whatever-it-is."

Saul tutted. "Don't you think you've had enough, Melissa?"

She wagged a finger at him. "Now, now, my good man. Don't go all macho on me. Remember who's the boss around here. For another week or two, anyway."

A light tap on the door interrupted them. Zoe poked her head around it. "Sorry, Miss Beecham. There's a call on the line."

"Tell them I'm out. Tell them I'm running naked through the streets while Rome burns. No, that was fiddling, wasn't it? I tell you what, Zoe, tell them to fuck off."

Zoe didn't quite know where to look. But she knew what to say. "No, it's not for you, Miss Beecham. It's for Mr Benton. An Abigail Miller for you, sir."

Saul choked back a grunt. "Abi? What does she want now?" He saw Melissa reach for the bottle. "Wait. No more. I'll be back in a minute. Just no more, ok?"

She saluted him with fingertips against forehead, only for them to make a V-shape as soon as he turned his back.

He picked up the call from Zoe's desk, covered the mouthpiece while he asked the PA to keep an eye on the CEO, took a deep breath, and spoke. "This is Saul Benton speaking. How can I help?"

"You can help by not messing with my daughter's head, that's how you can help. By leaving her alone. By crawling back under your stone."

"Whoa, whoa. That's enough. I'm not taking crap from you."

"Yes you are, Saul. I know about you and the boss-lady. Steph told me all about it last night. After I'd passed on your message. Love her? You only love yourself."

Saul dug fingers into the palm of his hand to stop him yelling down the line. Calmly, he said, "Abi, you're both wrong. There is absolutely nothing going on. A lift home, that was all. My reputation may go before me, but I love Steph. Love and respect her."

"Yada yada yada. So, if you love her, send her back."

"What do you mean 'send her back'? Send her back where?"

He felt the ice in her voice down the line. "To me. Send her and the little one inside her back to me."

"Abi, I can't send her back when she's already there."

There was a long silence. "You mean you haven't seen her?"

"No."

Another silence. "She set off first thing this morning. Her head's all over the place. Said she was going to tell you once-and-for-all. You've no future. That's what she was going to do. Four hours ago."

The elevator doors opened. Cyrus raced out. Almost knocked Saul flying. Gave an animated indication that he should follow him into Melissa's office.

Saul nodded. Mouthed 'I'm on the phone.' "Listen, Abi, I've got to go. Steph's a grown woman. She'll be shopping for baby clothes or something."

"But she's not answering her phone."

Saul tried to keep the exasperation out of his voice. "There's no reception in Elton Plaza. When she gets out, she'll ring you. Abi: I haven't seen her, but she's fine. I know it. Relax. Now, I've got to go."

He replaced the receiver, shook his head at it, and followed Cyrus Dilley into Melissa's office.

**

Saul was wrong. Steph Benton wasn't fine.

The room was cold. The floor was cold. She was cold. She shivered so much convulsions ran through her like waves.

Steph cradled her bump with her one free hand. "We'll get through this, Roland," she cooed. "I don't know what 'this' is yet, but well get through it. Trust me, I'm your Mum."

Those words opened the floodgates. Tears fell in torrents. Hollow, breathless sobs rent the cavernous room. She'd done all the screaming and the shouting. Tears were all she had left.

Until she set eyes on a pile of rags. And a blowtorch. And a can of petroleum.

She found more screams. She knew what 'this' was.

**

Saul re-entered Melissa's office in time to see her run a hand down her face. "Tell us what you've got," she was saying. Her voice remained slurred and her eyes glassy as marbles, but her head was clear.

Cyrus fidgeted with the fingers of one hand. The other held leaves of paper which he waved in the air. "I'm certain we're seeing two separate events here. On one hand, Pole Star are in our systems. They've manipulated EcoHug's accounts, secreted what is rightfully ours into their balance sheets. I've tracked money transfers. Pole Star are receiving deposits – and I mean massive deposits - from accounts across the globe. Cayman Islands, Nauru, and Samoa, mainly."

"So, they're syphoning our profits to tax havens before redirecting them across to their own?"

"Precisely. Then, they infiltrate our systems and those of our bank and manipulate our accounts. It's as if none of it ever touched EcoHug."

Melissa slapped her desk. "We've got them bang to rights. Brilliant work, Cyrus. Brilliant."

"Apart from one thing," Cyrus added. "We can't use any of what I've told you because what I did was illegal. And the killings mean EcoHug's in enough trouble already."

Saul joined the conversation. "Not if Pole Star are behind those, too, to discredit us." He looked towards Melissa. "That's your theory isn't it?"

Before she could speak, Dilley said, "They're not. At least, I've no evidence. I had Szydlowski run a search on every call made from all EcoHug plants over the last three months. It showed nothing unusual."

Saul wasn't convinced and said so. "Come on, man. Think about it. They wouldn't use a work's phone. It'd be a personal phone. A mobile, more than likely."

Dilley avoided eye contact but was firm in his response. "They haven't."

"And you can be sure, how?"

Dilley looked sheepish. "Because I devised a bug that let me check the personal phone records of every employee of EcoHug, via the systems of their own home and mobile providers. The program showed nothing untoward."

Saul let out a low whistle. "You're a nosey bastard, aren't you?"

Melissa stood by the window, watching over the rain-splashed city's streets. "The killer really is one of us."

A silence hung over them like a shroud. At length, Saul broke it. "My money's still on Pritchard."

"It's not Mr Pritchard." Cyrus's voice was firm. "I've looked at the images again."

"Don't tell me: they're fascinating," Saul said.

"As a matter of fact, they are. They prove Mr Pritchard didn't attack the girl. Mr Pritchard's right-handed. The images demonstrate the girl's wounds were caused by a weapon held in the left hand."

**

Zoe brought a tray laden with coffee. She'd done it for Melissa's benefit, to flush out the alcohol, but it afforded the threesome time to gather their thoughts. When Cyrus nipped to the bathroom, Melissa asked Saul about Abi Miller's telephone call. He barked a laugh. Told her Abi was paranoid. It was much ado about nothing. Crossed wires.

Cyrus returned. He looked troubled. Melissa spotted it. "You concerned about something, Cyrus? Are we missing something?"

He shook his head. He couldn't afford to make another mistake. He had to be sure.

Melissa took his response at face value. "I take it you haven't been able to pin down the origin of the e-mails?"

The IT man paused so long, Melissa thought he hadn't heard her. "Cyrus?"

"No. But," he struggled to meet her gaze, "There's been another."

Saul and Melissa made a noise like a sack of air deflating.

"Poor Patsy. He'll be mortified."

"It wasn't Mr MaGill's mail."

Two heads snapped towards him. "Huh?"

"It was amongst yours, Mr Benton."

**

The wind howled through cracked windows. Raindrops gathered on damaged sills, dripping the monotonous tears a cuckolded lover onto the bare floor. Darkness peered in, the light of a rising gibbous moon unable to penetrate the grime on the window.

Steph stared at the combustible material in the corner. She tore her eyes away, studied the walls, tried to make sense of the nonsense words and phrases scrawled on it.

Pain wracked her back. Her wrist, tethered to clasps on the wall, bruised and bled. Her other hand still rested on Roland, shielding him from what was to come.

And she had a pain. She needed a bathroom. She knew she wouldn't get to use one. Embarrassed to the core, she felt her bladder empty.

With a gush.

She knew it wasn't her bladder. Or urine.

"Oh no. Oh shit. I'm only twenty-six weeks. Shit, shit, shit."

She looked upwards and prayed.

"Please God. Not here. Not like this."

**

Cyrus Dilley fumbled with a print-out.

"Here it is. It doesn't say much."

Saul grabbed the sheet from him. Melissa craned her neck to see as Saul began reading.

"I had seen birth and death but had thought they were different."

He broke off, unable to read on. Melissa finished the quote for him. Without reading.

"This Birth was hard and bitter agony for us. Like Death, our death."

Saul's stomach plummeted into his scrotum at a rate of knots. Trembling fingers reached for his Samsung. His hands shook as he hit Abi's speed-dial button.

His heart beat like a jackhammer. He held his breath. The line went dead. Abi had rejected the call.

He dialled again. "You stupid, pretentious, self-centred, bitch. Pick the fucking thing up."

Realisation hit Melissa like breakers against a hull. She watched, hand on heart. Cyrus simply watched.

Abi Miller picked up at the third time of asking.

"Yes?" A tacit, cold question, spat out at him.

Saul held himself back, not wanting to worry 'the stupid, pretentious, self-centred bitch'. As calmly as he could, he asked one simple question.

"Hi Abi. Just wondering if Steph's home yet?"

The answer, simpler still, broke him.

**

Melissa did the only thing she knew. She filled a crystal tumbler with gin and passed it to the ashen-faced man. To her surprise, he accepted it. Knocked it back in one.

Saul gripped the crystal in his hand. "The bastard's going to die. I'm going to find him, chop his measly-little dick off and ram it down his throat." The words escaped through clenched teeth. "Jesus, he's going to pay. And I vow I'll do it before he lays a finger on Steph. I swear to God, I will."

Melissa heard the glass in Saul's hand crack. Saw scarlet ooze between the man's fingers. Drip onto the carpet. Saul hadn't noticed.

"Saul," she said. "Your hand."

He looked down. Gave the glass a final squeeze until it shattered. The blood came freely, now. But it seemed to galvanize Saul into action. "Are you with me?"

Melissa nodded, although she knew she was helpless.

He turned to Dilley, who watched the blood, mesmerised. "Will you help me? Use your kit to trace where she is?"

"I've already set a program running but there won't be time," he said, always the realist.

"Please, Cyrus. There must be something you can do."

"There is."

Saul waited for more. Nothing came. "What can you do, man?"

Cyrus looked Saul straight in the eye.

"I can tell you who it is."

THE WORST OF DAYS

"Help me. Somebody; help me. Please."

What started as a series of frantic shouts dimmed to a barely-audible whisper. Steph knew no-one was coming. No-one to help her, anyway. Tears flowed again. She tried to contain them, but couldn't. They ran down her face and dropped to the floor where they mingled with her amniotic fluid.

Her anti-natal class had mentioned something called PROM, but it had seemed so far off, she hadn't paid attention. She did remember she had to stay calm. She laughed through the tears. "I bet whoever said that's never been chained to a wall with a load of pyrotechnics at their feet."

She tried to recall anything else she'd been told. Remembered hearing it could be days, yet.

Or minutes.

Steph hoped it was days. If it was, it meant she'd lived through whatever the crazy had planned for her.

**

"Don't be so fucking stupid."

Saul had Dilley up against the wall, a fistful of T-shirt bunched up in his hands and fury in his voice.

"I haven't got time for silly-arse theories, Dilley. If you can't come up with anything better, fuck off back down to your Batcave until you do."

"Mr Benton, I assure you I don't deal in 'silly-arsed theories', as you put it. I look at the facts and apply a probability algorithm to them."

The calm, detached way he delivered the words pushed Saul over the cliff-edge. Despite his wounded hand, he powered a short-arm uppercut to the man's jaw. Upper and lower mandible collided with seismic force, tongue-tip trapped between them. Fragments of shattered teeth flew from Dilley's mouth. His jaw lolled open. Scarlet filled the maw.

Dilley's fingers pinched. Around Saul's testicles. Benton swore. Hesitated momentarily while in the grip of pain. Saul prepared to deliver another blow but found his arm seized. "Let go, Melissa, or I swear I'll hit you, too, if I have to."

She swung the gin bottle at his rib-cage. Knocked the wind out of him. He turned to the CEO, prepared to strike with bloodied, open palm.

"Stop!"

Even in his rage, he recognised the authority in her voice.

"Stop, Saul. Listen to him. Ok, just listen to him. What harm can it do to listen to him? Give him five minutes."

They watched Dilley spit remains of teeth and tongue and thick dollops of blood onto the cream carpet.

Slowly, Saul lowered his hand. Dilley released the grip on his ball-sack at the same leisurely pace.

"I'm thorry, Mr Benton," Cyrus lisped. "I know it mutht be difficult for you." He spat out more gore from his mouth. "But I'm thurtain ath I can be."

Saul fixed him with a stare. "You've said that before. Those exact words."

Cyrus nodded. "I know. And that'th why I didn't thay anything until now."

He spat again. Melissa handed him a glass of water. Dilley swilled it around his mouth. Dribbled more onto the carpet. Tenderly massaged his jaw. His speech improved. "But now he's got your wife. I can't hold back what I know."

Saul rubbed his temples. Tried to get his brain to work. It couldn't. He needed it spelt out for him.

"Ok. Ok. Make it quick. None of the War and Peace shit. Tell me why the killer's Patsy MaGill."

**

The contractions hadn't started yet but Steph knew they would. 'Minutes or days', she remembered.

With her free hand, she tried to mop up the fluid around her. She only had her dress to use. It soon became soaked. She sat in her own wetness.

"Hold on, Roland. Hold on, my love. Mummy will get us out. Just stay where you are. Don't come out. Please."

Roland responded with a kick. She patted her stomach. "You understand, don't you? There's a good boy. One kick for yes, two for no."

Steph stopped the conversation with her unborn son. She'd heard something. Her baby stilled, too. They'd both heard it.

Echoes of footsteps far below. Below, but approaching. Fast. Their pace matched the blood-flow at her temples. As the steps quickened and neared, so did her pulse.

"Hello?" she said, her voice low. "Is someone there?" Louder this time.

The staircase fell silent.

"Will you help me, please? I can't move. And I'm having my baby. Please, help me."

The door opened with the force of a thunderclap.

Steph looked towards it.

She'd known all along.

It wasn't help.

It was The Rat.

**

Melissa and Dilley perched on the edge of the office sofa. Saul prowled like a caged tiger.

"First off, the killer and Saul are both left-handed," Cyrus said.

"What does that prove?" Saul asked as he moved.

"Nothing in itself. But it does reduce the list of candidates to 12% of the population."

Saul turned and ploughed another furrow. "Next."

"Mr MaGill's lied to us."

"How?" Benton's words came out clipped.

"He was an only child. There's no sister."

That got Saul's attention. "Makes sense. He's never mentioned her before."

"How do you know?" Melissa's question.

"I ran some rudimentary checks. It's not difficult. So, it poses two questions: why lie, and what was Mr MaGill up to while on care leave?"

Saul grabbed a handful of his own hair. "Anything else?"

"There is."

"For fuck's sake man, what?"

"He's had treatment for a psychotic episode. Recently. His name's listed amongst clients of two self-help groups and a telephone counselling service."

Melissa prickled. "Proves nothing." It came out defensively, her own troubles to the fore.

"True. That's why I haven't said anything so far. It's all circumstantial. I was wrong once before. Can't afford to be wrong again." He wiped his hand across his mouth. Blood smeared his cheek and coated the back of his hand.

Concentration wrote itself across Saul's face. "When was this?"

"Around the time he returned to work after his surgery."

Saul made a dismissive sound. "And I don't blame him. Anyone would have trouble dealing with a cancer diagnosis. Your probability algorithm's based on shit, Dilley. We're wasting time here."

"I'm not finished." Again, he made the effort of maintaining eye contact.

Saul looked as if he was about to explode. "Don't wait for permission to speak, man. It's my wife he's got."

Melissa spoke in mellow tones. "Cyrus, can I ask a question first? Why would Patsy send himself e-mails, and then send one to Saul."

Cyrus thought it through, one eye on Saul's fist while he hesitated. "Firstly, to deflect attention from himself. It worked. You all sympathised with him."

Melissa thought of Patsy's reaction when he received the first e-mail. Was it over-reaction?

"I don't have an answer for your second question. All I know is, he had time to send it before we re-assembled here. And, who knows, perhaps he wants to be caught?"

Saul struggled with the mounting evidence. All circumstantial. No silver-bullet. Until Cyrus finished his theory.

"Possibly," Dilley said, "For the same reason he's been telephoning himself."

"What?" Melissa and Saul together.

"Szydlowski ran her eye over the telephone inventory a second time. She found an anomaly she missed first time. Someone was calling the same number at the same time each day. A call from Patsy MaGill. To Patsy MaGill. Not Mr MaGill's mobile number or his home number. The same number he was dialling out from."

The 'conference calls'. Saul swore. Loudly. "Find out where the Irish bastard is," he hissed.

Melissa reached for her desk phone. She'd dialled 99 when Saul ripped the cable from the socket.

"Saul, we've got to get the police onto this. It's your wife."

"Exactly. The police won't have any more idea where she is than we do. What's more, it'll take us too long to explain. They won't believe us unless we tell them everything. Then, they'll probably arrest us before doing anything to find Steph."

He looked over the city, "She's out there, somewhere. We do this ourselves."

A band on Dilley's wrist buzzed. He touched the screen. Scrolled his fingers upwards. Whistled. "My, we're in luck. My program's used the image of the murdered girl to plot the dimensions of the room she's in against a blueprint of every building in the city."

They looked at him expectantly.

"It's found her."

If they harboured any doubts about his theory, his next words dismissed them.

"It's on The Gallows estate. The old EcoHug building."

**

"We'll take the bike. It'll get through the traffic easier." Melissa grabbed the helmets and keys. Saul grabbed her wrist.

"You ride pillion. You've had three-quarters of a bottle of gin."

She felt sober as a judge, but he was right. "Cyrus, get down below. Find out anything that might help us. You know where we'll be, and you've got our numbers."

Dilley held his jaw together as he nodded. He dashed to the elevator with them. Stayed in for an additional floor after they'd alighted.

Saul trailed Melissa along by the wrist. She kicked off her shoes. Cold rainwater soaked her feet but she could keep up with Saul without them.

"Where's the bike?"

"In the shed to the right."

Neither were conscious of breathing but the loud rasps indicated they were. Saul jumped onto the Kawasaki, putting his weight on the pedal as Beecham wrapped her legs astride the seat and grabbed his waist.

The engine didn't fire. He tried again. Still nothing.

"You need to set the kill-switch to RUN," Melissa shouted in his ear.

"What the fuck's one of them?"

Beecham reached around him. Operated the switch.

He tried again. The engine fired. The Kawasaki lurched forward and stopped dead.

"Fuck," he yelled.

"You've never ridden one of these before, have you?"

"No, but I've got my bicycle proficiency certificate. Can't be much different once we're up and running."

Beecham rolled her eyes beneath her helmet. "Ok. Right. Start again. Make sure the gear shifter's in neutral this time. That's it. Now, squeeze the clutch leaver all the way to the grip. That's the one in your left hand."

This time, the engine kept going. The Kawasaki leapt forward like a kangaroo on speed. Melissa's head crunched between Saul's shoulder-blades. The bike snaked an S-shape but remained upright.

They roared out into traffic, soon up to forty mph, still in first gear.

Saul zig-zagged through the evening traffic, squeezed between cars at lights, leapt onto the pavement if they glared red.

Horns tooted, people dove for cover, others reached for their camera phones. They didn't hang around long enough to be identified.

The bike was doing ninety on rain-slicked surfaces. "Keep off the white lines," Melissa screamed at him. "Don't hit a line or you'll have us over." Her words streamed away behind her like a kite's tail.

As they approached The Gallows estate, traffic dwindled to nothing, the way birds hush at an eclipse. Saul slewed the Kawasaki to a halt outside the boarded-up entrance, spilling them off as the bike toppled onto its side.

He was on his feet in an instant, heaving at the shutters, screaming Steph's name. A gap appeared, he squeezed through, a sharp edge tore his ear, and then he was in.

Melissa barrelled into him. He'd stopped dead

"Jesus H Christ. Will you look at that?"

**

Cyrus Dilley hunched over the keyboards in the cramped space where he was most at home. He was astonished – and not a little perturbed – how unprotected the system was. Once in, it was even simpler to find what he was after.

Cyrus rocked back in his chair. It wasn't in his make-up to swear, but he, too, said, "Jesus H Christ, will you look at that?"

He reached for his phone. No answer. Concrete and cement building. No infrastructure at the receiving end. No signal.

Dilley dashed up one flight stairs, out into the rain and a waiting cab.

**

They stood in the former lobby of the decrepit EcoHug building. Stripped of its furnishings and contents, it bore no more resemblance to its former life than the body of a corpse captures the spirit of the soul it once held.

But it wasn't the empty space that held them rapt. It was the walls. Every inch, as far as an arm could reach, was covered in graffiti. Lurid colours, sweeping curved arcs; this was not the roughly-hewn scrawl of a local drop-out. This was more Banksy than angsty.

"Dilley was right," Melissa whispered. "This is the place. The writing. It's quotes from Eliot." She turned 360 degrees. "All of it."

An icicle ran down Saul's spine. "Come on, I've a wife to find. And she's not on this floor."

They found a staircase. Placed their backs against the wall and made their way upwards, checking each turn as they went. The stone wall grazed their backs as the climbed. They stopped to listen. Nothing.

The second floor – the former executive floor – was the only one of cellular design. No open space here. Several smaller, independent rooms. It'd be like searching the honeycomb of a hive to find the Queen.

They chose not to split up. They didn't speak to one another. Communicated by hand signals, like cops in a TV show. At each door, Saul took one side, Melissa the other. Each was empty.

When there were only three left to check, Saul heard a noise. Not much, but enough for him to halt and raise a finger to his lips. They listened. Nothing but silence.

Saul lowered the finger from his lips. Just as he prepared to set off, he heard the sound again. Melissa nodded. She'd heard it, too.

They crawled towards its source, stealthy as leopards.

Melissa and Saul reached the doorway just as someone stepped out. Saul lowered his head and barrelled into the man's stomach. Slammed the man against the wall. Heard air explode from his lungs.

The man slumped to the floor, a baseball cap knocked askew.

All Saul's emotions poured out in a violent fury. Kicks broke more of the man's ribs and shattered nasal cartilage. Fingers crunched beneath vicious stamps, so did shinbone. Saul wouldn't stop. He couldn't stop. Patsy – his friend – had to suffer the way his actions had hurt him.

The man at his feet rolled over. Abject fear showed in his eyes.

Saul stopped mid-kick.

They weren't the eyes of Patsy MaGill.

They were the eyes of Victor Pritchard.

THE END OF DAYS

Cyrus Dilley had found the only cab driver who obeyed both traffic regulations and the Highway Code. Dilley constantly checked his watch. Drummed his feet against the cab floor. Opened and closed his fingers.

The driver kept glancing in the rear-view mirror. "You all right, mate?"

A reflex action took Dilley's hand to his missing teeth and slack jaw. "Concentrate on the road, please. I need to get there quickly."

Traffic lightened as they approached The Gallows. The cab's lights swept round bends like searchlights, catching in pools of water, reflecting back in their eyes. They passed the bent and damaged marker signalling the start of the old industrial estate.

Tall buildings, the corpse of Britain's long-deceased industry, towered over the cab like tombstones in a cemetery. Another mile and he'd be there.

And then the cab pulled into a lay-by.

"We're not there yet."

"We are, mate. At least, I am. I'm not going any further. You know what goes on further up the estate. I've got my licence to think of. This is as far as I go."

Dilley swore again. Twice in half an hour. He paid the fare and set off on foot in the pouring rain.

**

"Give me one good reason why I shouldn't spatchcock you right here, right now."

Vic the Prick shrank from him. "Stop him, Miss Beecham. Please. Make him stop." The lower half of his face was caked in blood from his ruptured nose. The man was crying.

"Answer his question, Pritchard."

"I would if I knew what I was supposed to have done," Pritchard cowered.

Saul placed his foot against the remains of Pritchard's nose. "One last chance. What have you done with my wife, you rat."

"Your wife? Nothing. I haven't seen her since she came to the office looking for you. Honest."

"Really? That the best you can do? All right, you snivelling, perverted bastard, in that case, tell me what you're doing here."

Pritchard eased himself away from Benton's boot as it hovered over his head. He cried in pain as his broken leg twisted. His breath came in short, whistling, rasps.

"I wanted to know what he was doing. I saw him on a bench a few hours ago. Thought he looked a bit odd. Not quite with it. So, I followed him. I lost him for a long while. I'd given up. I kept on walking." He coughed up blood. Lots of it. "Ended up around here. That's when I saw him again, sneaking into this place."

Saul asked a superfluous question.

"Who?"

"Patsy MaGill. I was looking for him when you jumped me."

Saul was half-way to the next floor before Pritchard finished speaking.

**

Melissa flew up the staircase after him. She stubbed her toe on a stair. Cried out in pain. Picked up the trail of blood left by Saul's hand. She hopped through a gap which once housed a door.

And saw Steph Benton.

Saul had also seen her. While he stood transfixed by the scene, Melissa knew immediately what had happened. "God, Saul. Her waters have broken."

Saul came out of his trance. "Steph. Are you alright?"

Tears flowed down her face like a waterfall. "Yes. No. I don't know. Just get me out of here." She nodded her head in the direction of the pyre.

"Shit a brick."

"Saul. Look at the wall above her head."

He did. "What am I looking for?"

"The inscription."

He read it.

'The only hope, or else despair
Lies in the choice of pyre or pyre –
To be redeemed from fire by fire.'

Melissa explained. "It's from The Fire Sermon."

Saul couldn't take it in. "My God. MaGill was going to burn her alive."

He took two paces towards her. Then stopped dead in his tracks when a figure emerged through a doorway next to Steph. Patsy MaGill. Carrying kindle and another blowtorch. Which he pointed at Steph Benton's head.

**

Patsy smiled warmly at them. "Hello Saul. Miss Beecham. What are you doing here?"

"What do you think I'm doing? I'm here for my wife."

"Oh good. As you'll see, she's fine. A bit wet, but fine."

Saul clenched his fists. Every muscle in his body contracted like a coiled spring. He looked at the blowtorch in MaGill's hand. "Put that down."

"What, this little thing?" He waved it in the air. "I don't think so. I need it. In case she comes back."

Melissa clung to Saul. "In case who comes back?" she asked.

He laughed. "Isn't it obvious? My sister."

Saul and Melissa exchanged glances.

"You haven't got a sister."

MaGill spoke slowly, detached. "Of course I have. Who do you think's responsible for this? I couldn't let her do anything to Steph. So, I'm here to set her free."

"Patsy. Listen to me. We know you don't have a sister. But let me have Steph. Let her go." Saul inched towards him.

"I'm sorry, I can't. It's too dangerous. She'll be back any minute. I can feel it."

Melissa whispered to Saul. "He's completely crazy. Cyrus was right. About everything."

Their attention was distracted by a commotion in the doorway. Cyrus Dilley burst through, bloodied and breathless.

"I'm afraid I wasn't right about everything. Mr MaGill has indeed got a sister. A twin sister."

**

Saul and Melissa couldn't take it in. "But you said…"

"I know I did. But I've found out a lot of things in the last hour."

Patsy let out a howl of triumph. "Thank you, Cyrus. Now, please trust me. Let me handle Patricia when she gets here."

"Patricia? Fuck me," Saul said. "No, we're not hanging around. We're getting out of here now, while we can."

They'd been so focused on Patsy they'd taken their eyes off Steph. Missed all the subliminal signs she gave them. With a blowtorch pointed at her temple, she daren't speak.

"It's too late. She's here." Patsy's voice.

Patsy turned to face the door he'd stepped from. When he turned back, he was wooden, eyes glassy. *"What do you think you're doing here?"* The voice was strained, higher-pitched, an eerie far-away lilt which made the hackles rise on everyone in the room.

Patsy's normal voice returned. "Leave them, Patricia. They're my friends."

"Friends? You call these ragamuffins friends? Look at them." The odd voice again. *"Who's the woman?"* the tone bitter, full of hatred.

"That's Melissa. She's my CEO."

The other four in the room froze, chilled to the bone. Saul whispered to Melissa, "Fucking hell. He's having a conversation with himself."

"He's completely flipped. It's as if he's possessed," Melissa hissed through her teeth.

Cyrus spoke. "He is, in a way. Let me handle this."

Saul looked at him wide-eyed. "No fucking chance. We need a trained negotiator for this. Or a priest. Someone tactful. Someone who knows what they're doing. You're as tactful as a fart in a lift."

Melissa laid a hand on Saul's arm. Spoke in his ear. "Let him speak. He knows something. Trust him."

Cyrus continued. Calmly. Hypnotically. "Do you know who I am?"

Patsy / Patricia's head tilted, considering.

"My name's Cyrus."

"Ah yes. You're the different one, aren't you? I'm pleased to meet you."

"And me, you." Patricia stared at Cyrus who, with a painful effort, retained eye contact. "I've read a lot about you."

"You have?"

"Yes. Quite unique, aren't you?"

"You might be clever. But you don't know ANYTHING about me."

"Would you like to tell me about yourself, then?"

"That depends. It depends whether you want to know about me, or The Rat. I assure you The Rat has a much more interesting tale to tell." The falsetto laugh made all but Cyrus shudder.

Saul began edging away from the group as Cyrus spoke again.

"Who's The Rat? Was it The Rat who killed Kerri?"

"The Rat and I are one and the same. Or should I say two and the same." The ghostly laugh again. *"And, of course we killed Kerri. Who else could it be?"*

Saul almost launched himself at the thing, there and then, but he kept his focus on the fuel canister and the second blowtorch. He inched further away. Towards it. Melissa couldn't look. She couldn't even breathe.

Benton moved another few feet.

"I saw what The Rat did to the other girl. It fascinated me. I'd love to know how you did it."

The Rat's eyes flared. *"Which one? There's been so many. Ah yes. The little China girl. The best yet, don't you think?"* The Rat glanced down at Steph. Waved the blowtorch in her face. *"I have high hopes for this one, though."*

Steph stared into the blower. "Please. My baby."

Saul couldn't let his fear get the better of him. He took another step, out of range of The Rat's peripheral vision.

"Yes, it is such a shame about your child, I agree. Especially because it's a boy. However, c'est la vie." The unintentional irony brought another laugh.

Cyrus flexed his smashed jaw as he prepared to speak again. The Rat cut him off. *"Before you say any more, can I ask you something?"*

"Of course you can. You can ask me anything."

The voice hardened. The Rat's fingers touched the blowtorch's trigger. *"Can I ask you to tell the stupid bastard making his way across the room to get his arse back over here before I vaporise his wife's eyeballs?"*

Saul swore. Melissa and Steph sagged.

"In fact, you can also send the other slut over here as insurance. I'm sure she'd like to meet Patricia, too."

Melissa steeled herself. She walked towards The Rat determined to show no fear. Until The Rat grabbed her by the hair. Melissa's scalp caught fire, no torch or gasoline needed. The Rat dragged her across the floor to where the fuel can lay.

Saul sensed an opportunity. He took a half-step forwards Steph. A roar from the blowtorch stopped him dead. Flame belched inches above Melissa's head.

Benton raised his hands. Backtracked.

The Rat scraped the fuel can along the concrete floor with its foot, blowtorch in one hand, Melissa Beecham's hair in the other. All the while, it watched the men.

Once back beneath the graffiti inscription, The Rat dragged Melissa to her knees where she floundered in Steph Benton's waters. The women found the strength to smile at each other in solidarity. The women's fingers interlocked.

Saul couldn't move. He was paralyzed by fear. He sought solace in the eyes of Steph and Melissa but received only panic as a reward.

Panic, and something else.

Steph lowered her head to her knees. Screwed her eyes tight. Let rip a terrifying, high-pitched mewl.

Melissa knew straight away. She'd felt Steph's grip tighten like a vice on her hand. "A contraction. She's started. The baby's on its way."

Saul took two steps towards his wife. A burst of flame licked his arm, singed his flesh, but still he moved forward. Until The Rat extinguished the flame and set the tip of the blower against his wife's cheek. Steph yelled in agony as her face blistered beneath the hot tip.

"I think it's time you men left. I really don't want you to witness this." The haunting voice circled in the air like a vulture awaiting death.

Cyrus remained calm. "Thank you for the warning, Patricia. I appreciate it. Do you think I could speak with Patsy before we go?"

"We're not going anywhere. Not without the girls." Saul's voice wavered but he'd never been more certain of anything.

Cyrus gave him a thin-lipped smile. Feigned wiping blood from his mouth. Said "I know we're not" behind the shield of his hand.

"I know why you're doing this, Patricia. You think these women you've killed, and the ones you've yet to slay, they've wasted their life, haven't they? A life you could live so much better than they."

"I like you, Mr Dilley. You see things others don't."

Cyrus's head thumped from the effort of keeping eye contact with The Rat. It hurt so much more than his jaw.

"Thank you," he said, the tone more mesmeric. "I'd like the chance to explain to Mr MaGill before we leave you to your task, if I can. He worries about you, and it might help him accept your actions if I could speak with him."

The Rat studied him with cold, dead eyes. *"Very well. But I'm still here. Remember that, won't you? I may like you but you're not going to stop me. None of you are."*

A brief but violent tremor surged through The Rat. Then, it's eyes flickered.

"Patsy?"

"Hello, Cyrus."

Saul's stomach lurched at the transformation. Bile rose in his throat. He glanced towards Steph and Melissa who looked on open-mouthed.

Steph's face crumpled. Her free hand sprung away from Melissa's and she held her stomach as the pain gripped her. "Jee-zus". Another contraction swept through her.

"Are you alright, Steph?" Patsy asked.

Saul replied for his wife. "She's having my baby, idiot. In this filthy midden. All because of you."

He raised a fist. Cyrus held him back. "Don't. The Rat will return."

"Who's The Rat? I hope you're not referring to Patricia. Please don't confuse her with The Rat."

"Of course not, Patsy," Cyrus said. "Now, can I have a word with you? About your operation. You remember, don't you?"

Patsy laughed. "You don't forget a thing like cancer."

"It wasn't cancer. You lied."

All heads turned to Cyrus.

"Didn't you?"

Patsy looked to the floor. Laid a hand on his abdomen. "I said it was benign. It was malignant. That was the only lie."

Cyrus looked around the room, at the graffiti-strewn walls, blood stains, manacles and chains. He looked at Steph and Melissa. At a near-broken Saul. "It was most definitely malignant," he said, "But it wasn't a tumour, was it?"

"What do you mean? Of course it was."

Steph let rip with an urgent groan. Another contraction. Melissa spoke. "Cyrus, we don't have long."

He nodded. Looked at Steph for a long while. Asked Patsy a question while he watched her. "Have you heard of something called fetus in fetu, Mr MaGill?"

Patsy cast his head down.

"I'm sure you have, but I'll remind you anyway. You and Patricia, if she's listening. Fetus in fetu is a rare condition. It affects less than one in a half million. But you were one of those. It occurs in pregnancy. With twins who share a placenta."

The concrete chamber fell silent, the only sound rain rattling against the windows and Patsy's raspy breathing.

"One twin wraps itself around the other. Develops around it. Envelopes it so the engulfed twin becomes a parasite. Its survival depends on its host twin. The parasitic twin may have a few shrivelled internal organs but is always anencephalic. It never has a brain."

The air became icy cold. Saul, Melissa and Steph's flesh puckered like a turkey's. The listened, rapt. Another contraction came and went, then another.

"The host twin feeds the enveloped twin. Cares for it. Nurtures it. Just as you cared and nurtured Patricia"

Patsy MaGill shook his head. "No. That's not right. It can't be right."

"Mr MaGill, it is right. You know it is. You also know the twin dies. It always dies. When it's discovered, often decades later, it must be removed."

Shudders of revulsion seized Saul, Steph and Melissa, but they convulsed

Patsy more than any other.

"And that's why you were in hospital, and why you struggled to cope afterwards. You didn't have a tumour removed. You had your dead twin removed. Patricia's dead, Patsy. She can't hurt you, or anyone else ever again."

Patsy's eyes flickered. He stiffened. The Rat was back.

"'SHE' is not dead. 'SHE' is still here." Evil lurked in the black depths of its eyes. Evil and madness. *"'SHE' is the cat's mother. The mother who read to us in the womb, in the crib, at her knee. She'd read to us about Macavity, Skimbleshanks and Mr Mistoffelees."*

Melissa understood. "Old Possum. TS Eliot. The quotes."

"Very clever, for a horse-faced bitch. Now, let me see what the horse makes of this one." The Rat closed its eyes. Its nostrils flared. And it recited:

"The communication of the dead is tongued with fire beyond the language of the living'."

The Rat twisted the cap off the fuel canister. Raised the can above the heads of Steph and Melissa. They screamed. Melissa threw herself over Steph, shielding her, as The Rat began to tip the canister. They heard the blowtorch fire up.

And heard Patsy's voice yell, "No."

"It has to be. Let them burn."

"You can't. They're my friends. Good friends. I love them."

"You love me more."

"You don't fucking exist."

Patsy tipped the contents of the canister over his head.

The girls heard a whoosh as flame ignited the kerosene. They felt incandescent heat. Smelt burning flesh. But they felt no agony.

They looked up. Saw Patsy mouth, 'I'm sorry' before his agonized, shrill screams doused all other sound.

Saul wanted to cry out, too, but he was struck mute. He tried to turn his back but was transfixed.

He craved darkness behind closed, teary eyes where a monochrome, silent world lay without the blood and the flames and the desperate screams of his friend, Patsy MaGill.

SUNDAY AUGUST 12ᵀᴴ
THE BEST OF DAYS

Cotton bud clouds floated in a denim-blue sky. A ripened-peach of a sun beat down on the cathedral, its stained glass reflecting tints and sparkles like fairy lights on a Christmas tree. It was a Laurie Lee kind of day in a Ken Loach kind of city.

From a discrete distance, Melissa and Cyrus looked on as Saul and Steph spoke to the Dean. Saul held Roland Kerry Benton in his arms while his wife smoothed the infant's christening robe.

Melissa wore a lighter shade of blue than the heavens; short skirt below a lightweight matching jacket. She'd wound a cream scarf around her head turban-style to disguise the A5-sized patch of scalp her doctor warned would probably never sport hair.

Alongside her, Cyrus wore his only suit - a shabby grey affair - over his omnipresent T-shirt. He'd made an effort; the T-shirt was white, not black.

"He's lovely, isn't he?" Melissa asked.

"Who?"

"The baby, silly. Who else?"

Cyrus offered no words. His smirk said everything for him.

"Detective Sergeant Nawaz called last night," Melissa said, eyes on the happy parents. "They've formally closed their enquiries. EcoHug's clear. As far as they're concerned, Patsy's the only one involved. They reached the conclusion he couldn't come to terms with the...", she struggled to remember the term.

"Fetus in fetu."

"Yes, fetus in fetu. It pushed him over the edge of insanity. Took it out on people he knew. Kerri. Steph. No explanation as to why he killed the other."

"Others, plural," Cyrus corrected.

"No. The other. They only know for certain of one other. No need to let them think otherwise."

"Good. And they're right, as it happens. Mr MaGill would never do such things. The killer really WAS the fetus in fetu. The killer, The Rat, was Patricia; not Patsy."

Melissa's eyes brightened at the thought. "Thank you, Cyrus. That helps. A lot."

Dilley returned to his matter-of-fact ways. "All EcoHug's systems are clean. I wiped everything, disconnected the tracing tools, just about cleared my entire office before I quit. They'll never trace anything back to the company."

Melissa nodded. She squinted into the sun. After a while, she asked "What are you going to do now?"

Cyrus shrugged. "What about you?"

Melissa shrugged, too.

Saul spotted them. He pointed them out to Steph. Steph turned and waved, face creased with smiles. Melissa waved back. Saul handed Roland to his wife and, once safely snuggled in her arms, tenderly kissed the baby's forehead.

He dug his hands deep into his suit pockets and sauntered over to his erstwhile colleagues.

"So, the Three Musketeers, back together again," he said. "Thanks for coming. It can't have been easy for you."

"A lot easier than the last time I was here. Christenings are preferable to funerals."

They stood in silence, lost in their own personal memories of Patsy and his funeral.

Melissa changed the subject. "Cyrus and I were just talking about what we do next."

"The million dollar question. We still need to nail Pole Star for the financial shenanigans."

"You forget, Saul - you're the only one who works for them now."

Saul thought for a moment. "You know, we make a good team. We should do something together. The three of us."

He let the thought ferment as he watched a car play hide and seek with the shadow of the Cathedral spire. It pulled up close to the narthex. Abigail Miller stepped out.

She took Roland from her daughter. Began strapping him into the car seat. Steph pointed out Saul to her. Abi gave a brusque nod in his direction. Steph and Abi climbed in. The car pulled away, snaked along the gravel road, and was gone.

Saul remembered something he'd read on a wall in a Gallows Estate building. Softly, he recited,

"'What we call the beginning is often the end. And to make an end is to make a beginning. The end is where we start from."

Melissa wrapped her arms around Saul's waist, an echo of the EcoHug logo, and laid her head on his shoulder.
"Come on. Let's go home."

ABOUT THE AUTHOR

Colin Youngman is a true Geordie (born within sound of the tugboats on the River Tyne), and now lives in Northumberland, north-east England.

His first work was published at the age of 9 when a contribution to children's comic Sparky brought him the rich rewards of a 10/- Postal Order and a transistor radio. Since then, his material has featured in outlets as diverse as national newspapers, sports magazines, and travel guides, all whilst developing a career as a Senior Executive in the Public Sector.

Colin now writes thriller / mystery novels and novellas with trademark twists designed to hit you like a kick in the guts.

He also works as a TV Supporting Artiste and has been approached for roles in ITV crime serial Vera and appeared in period drama Victoria. He has recently filmed an episode for series 3 of Netflix production Frontier.

Please leave a review on Amazon if you enjoyed this book.

Follow Colin on Twitter @seewhy59
and
Facebook (Colin.Youngman.Author).

Printed in Great Britain
by Amazon